LEO TOLSTOY

THE
KREUTZER
SONATA

Revised translation by Isai Kamen

Introduction by Doris Lessing

Notes by Dr. Michael A. Denner
STETSON UNIVERSITY

THE MODERN LIBRARY

NEW YORK

2003 Modern Library Paperback Edition

Introduction copyright © 2003 by Doris Lessing
Notes and reading group guide copyright © 2003 by Random House, Inc.
Biographical note copyright © 1994 by Random House, Inc.
Copyright © 1957, 1985 by Random House, Inc.

LIBRARY OF CONGRESS CATALOGING-IN-PUBLICATION DATA
Tolstoy, Leo, graf, 1828–1910.
[Kreitserova sonata. English]
The Kreutzer sonata / Leo Tolstoy ; revised translation by Isai Kamen ;
introduction by Doris Lessing ; notes by Michael A. Denner.
p.   cm.
ISBN 978-0-8129-6823-1
I. Kamen, Isai.   II. Denner, Michael A.   III. Title.
PG3366.K7   2003
891.73'3—dc21
2003051021

Modern Library website address: www.modernlibrary.com

Printed in the United States of America

LEO TOLSTOY

Count Lev (Leo) Nikolayevich Tolstoy was born on August 28, 1828, at Yasnaya Polyana (Bright Glade), his family's estate located 130 miles southwest of Moscow. He was the fourth of five children born to Count Nikolay Ilyich Tolstoy and Marya Nikolayevna Tolstoya (née Princess Volkonskaya, who died when Tolstoy was barely two). He enjoyed a privileged childhood typical of his elevated social class (his patrician family was older and prouder than the czar's). Early on, the boy showed a gift for languages as well as a fondness for literature—including fairy tales, the poems of Pushkin, and the Bible, especially the Old Testament story of Joseph. Orphaned at the age of nine by the death of his father, Tolstoy and his brothers and sister were first cared for by a devoutly religious aunt. When she died, in 1841, the family went to live with their father's only surviving sister in the provincial city of Kazan. Tolstoy was educated by French and German tutors until he enrolled at Kazan University in 1844. There he studied law and Oriental languages and developed a keen interest in moral philosophy and the writings of Rousseau. A notably unsuccessful student who led a dissolute life, Tolstoy abandoned his studies in 1847 without earning a degree and returned to Yasnaya Polyana to claim the property (along with 350 serfs and their families) that was his birthright.

After several aimless years of debauchery and gambling in Moscow and St. Petersburg, Tolstoy journeyed to the Caucasus in 1851 to join his older brother Nikolay, an army lieutenant participating in the Caucasian campaign. The following year Tolstoy officially enlisted in the military, and in 1854 he became a commissioned officer in the artillery, serving first on the Danube and later in the Crimean War. Although his sexual escapades and profligate gambling during this period shocked even his fellow soldiers, it was while in the army that Tolstoy began his literary apprenticeship. Greatly influenced by the works of Charles Dickens, Tolstoy wrote *Childhood,* his first novel. Published pseudonymously in September 1852 in the *Contemporary,* a St. Petersburg journal, the book received highly favorable reviews—earning the praise of Turgenev—and overnight established Tolstoy as a major writer. During the following years he contributed several novels and short stories (about military life) to the *Contemporary*—including *Boyhood* (1854), three Sevastopol stories (1855–1856), "Two Hussars" (1856), and *Youth* (1857).

In 1856 Tolstoy left the army and went to live in St. Petersburg, where he was much in demand in fashionable salons. He quickly discovered, however, that he disliked the life of a literary celebrity (he often quarreled with fellow writers, especially Turgenev) and soon departed on his first trip to western Europe. Upon returning to Russia, he produced the story "Three Deaths" and a short novel, *Family Happiness,* both published in 1859. Afterward, Tolstoy decided to abandon literature in favor of more "useful" pursuits. He retired to Yasnaya Polyana to manage his estate and established a school there for the education of children of his serfs. In 1860 he again traveled abroad in order to observe European (especially German) educational systems; he later published *Yasnaya Polyana,* a journal expounding his theories on pedagogy. The following year he was appointed an arbiter of the peace to settle disputes between newly emancipated serfs and their former masters. But in July 1862 the police raided the school at Yasnaya Polyana for evidence of subversive activity. The search elicited an indignant protest from Tolstoy directly to Alexander II, who officially exonerated him.

That same summer, at the age of thirty-four, Tolstoy fell in love with eighteen-year-old Sofya Andreyevna Bers, who was living with her parents on a nearby estate. (As a girl she had reverently memorized whole passages of *Childhood.*) The two were married on September 23, 1862, in a church inside the Kremlin walls. The early years of the marriage were largely joyful (thirteen children were born of the union) and coincided with the period of Tolstoy's great novels. In 1863 he not only published *The Cossacks,* but began work on *War and Peace,* his great epic novel, which came out in 1869.

Then, on March 18, 1873, inspired by the opening of a fragmentary tale by Pushkin, Tolstoy started writing *Anna Karenina.* Originally titled *Two Marriages,* the book underwent multiple revisions and was serialized to great popular and critical acclaim between 1875 and 1877.

It was during the torment of writing *Anna Karenina* that Tolstoy experienced the spiritual crisis that recast the rest of his life. Haunted by the inevitability of death, he underwent a "conversion" to the ideals of human life and conduct that he found in the teachings of Christ. *A Confession* (1882), which was banned in Russia, marked this change in his life and works. Afterward, he became an extreme rationalist and moralist, and in a series of pamphlets published during his remaining years Tolstoy rejected both church and state, denounced private ownership of property, and advocated celibacy, even in marriage. In 1897 he even went so far as to renounce his own novels, as well as many other classics, including Shakespeare's *Hamlet* and Beethoven's Ninth Symphony, for being morally irresponsible, elitist, and corrupting. His teachings earned him numerous followers in Russia ("We have two czars, Nicholas II and Leo Tolstoy," a journalist wrote) and abroad (most notably, Mahatma Gandhi) but also many opponents, and in 1901 he was excommunicated by the Russian holy synod. Prompted by Turgenev's deathbed entreaty ("My friend, return to literature!"), Tolstoy did produce several more short stories and novels—including the ongoing series *Stories for the People, The Death of Ivan Ilyich* (1886), *The Kreutzer Sonata* (1889), *Master and Man* (1895), *Resurrection* (1899), and *Hadji Murád* (published posthumously)—as well as a play, *The Power of Darkness* (1886).

Tolstoy's controversial views produced a great strain on his marriage, and his relationship with his wife deteriorated. "Until the day I die she will be a stone around my neck," he wrote. "I must learn not to drown with this stone around my neck." Finally, on the morning of October 28, 1910, Tolstoy fled by railroad from Yasnaya Polyana headed for a monastery in search of peace and solitude. However, illness forced Tolstoy off the train at Astapovo; he was given refuge in the stationmaster's house and died there on November 7. His body was buried two days later in the forest at Yasnaya Polyana.

THE
KREUTZER
SONATA

Contents

INTRODUCTION

Doris Lessing

Tolstoy was always in trouble with the censor and the czar's police. He was expected by the common people and the liberal opposition to take a stand—and he did—on every kind of humanitarian issue, from famines mishandled by the government to persecutions by an arbitrary and often cruel regime. He was known as much as a social critic and moralist as an author. "There are two czars in Russia," pronounced one liberal spokesman, "and the other is Tolstoy." He was described as the conscience of the world. This novel, published in 1889 when Tolstoy was sixty-one, caused instant scandal. The censor was going to ban it, but a compromise was reached by allowing it in an edition too expensive for ordinary people. Not that banning Tolstoy did much good: his works were copied out by disciples and distributed in hundreds of copies. Samizdat was not invented by the Soviets. (Samizdat was the illegal distribution of works banned by the Communist party.) Because of Tolstoy's moral authority it was not possible to ignore it or pretend that these unappetizing views were of no importance. In America, the U.S. Postal Service banned the mailing of newspapers serializing *The Kreutzer Sonata*. Theodore Roosevelt said that Tolstoy was a sexual moral pervert. The nascent women's movements were furious: this was the time of the New Woman. Chekhov, who revered Tolstoy, defended the book because of its aesthetic virtues and because, he said, the whole subject needed discussion. The emotional reactions to the novel have always been inordinate, but something written at white heat must provoke incandescent reactions. I think people reading it now will feel, first of all, curiosity—what was all that fuss about?—and then, almost certainly, disquiet, dismay, and incredulity that anything so wrongheaded could be written by a favorite author: *War and Peace, Anna Karenina, Resurrection.*

Reading it now, something has to strike you. The tale originated in a true story that was in all the newspapers and used by Tolstoy for polemic purposes. A husband did kill his wife out of jealousy, but the tale as told by Tolstoy makes you ask, "Wait a minute. But what, in fact, did this erring wife do?" Nothing much, even according to the stricter modes and morals of that time. A furor of suspicion and rage is built on atmospheres, glances, possibilities by a husband's jealous imagination. We may imagine her defending herself: "But, Your Honor, nothing happened! I have the misfortune to be married to a jealous maniac who made my life a misery. He himself introduced this man who is supposed to be my lover into our house and encouraged his visits to play music—we are both keen amateur musicians. The evening my husband returned unexpectedly and found me having supper with this supposed lover, I had thought that for once I could invite him around without being made to feel a criminal. Sir, nothing could have been more innocent. How could I possibly have done anything wrong? The servants were up, serving supper, and the children were awake and watching everything, the way children do. Nothing happened. Nothing could have happened." She never did get the chance to defend herself because her husband killed her in a jealous fury.

The novel could be read as a brilliant account of unjustified male jealousy. There could not be a better description of a man working himself up into jealous madness. It could be analyzed, and almost certainly has been, by psychiatrists, presenting it as a case history of latent homosexuality, textbook stuff, really.

It is useful to contrast the fevered voice of Tolstoy in *The Kreutzer Sonata* with *Anna Karenina,* a panoramic account of sexual and marital relations. In *Anna Karenina,* a newly married couple, Kitty and Levin, are just settling into their life together in the country. Levin is modeled on the young Tolstoy. He is described as eccentric in his social views, awkward in company, and immoderately in love with his wife. It is summer, the house is full of visitors, and one of them is a young man from the fashionable life that Levin (and Tolstoy) despises. He is a comic character, stout, wearing a ridiculous Scottish bonnet and streamers, is greedy, and he has a crush on Kitty. Flirting with her would be normal behavior in the Moscow and St. Petersburg salons, but Levin suffers and throws him out of the house. His worldly male relatives mock him and call him "a turk." Wonderfully observed are the absurd quarrels of the young couple, instigated always by the husband, who is ashamed of himself and cannot stop watching his imagined rival and putting the worst possible interpretation on everything he sees. Levin is seen as an oddball by family and neighbors—all those ridiculous ideas about the peasants and agriculture—and as foolishly jealous, but held in the sweep and power of that novel, when Levin throws the society peacock out of the house, Tolstoy's affectionate portrait tells us that he thinks Levin is no more than rather touchingly absurd. But the same author wrote *The Kreutzer Sonata.*

And Tolstoy wrote *War and Peace,* whose great quality is balance, the command of a panoramic sweep of events and people. That dispassionate eagle eye is nowhere here. What we have in *The Kreutzer Sonata* is the power and the energy but not the sanity of judgment. Tolstoy's position could not be more extreme, and in case anyone might imagine that he regretted *The Kreutzer Sonata,* he wrote an apologia, *Sequel to The Kreutzer Sonata,* sometime later, where he reiterated it all, like hammering nails into a coffin, burying any possibility of joy, enjoyment, even the mildest fun in sex, love, lovemaking. Yet the author of the two great novels describes all kinds of passion and enjoyment, the emotions that we sinful lesser mortals might associate with sex.

In the grip of his fanaticism, Tolstoy advocated chastity for the entire human race, and when it was objected that this would end the human race, his reply was the equivalent of "And so what!" Or rather, *tant pis,* as this member of a Francophile caste would have put it.

But he could not have believed in the possibility of chastity, for his own life taught him otherwise. His struggles with his sexuality are documented, and by himself, sometimes confusingly, not because he tried to conceal them, but because his behavior and his principles did not match.

Before marriage he was corrupt and debased—so he said. He slept around with peasant women, and there was at least one illegitimate child. There were always the Gypsies, too—rather, THE GYPSIES!—

always charming young men from the paths of virtue, and Tolstoy went off to the Gypsies, like so many of the characters from the novels of that time. After marriage, no Gypsies, and he tried hard to be a faithful husband. He was strongly sexed, going at it well into his seventies.

Late in his life Tolstoy became what we would call a born-again Christian. He had a religious experience which changed him. A type of religious conversion is described in *Anna Karenina*. Levin is in despair because he has no faith. It is hard for us now to understand this, unless it is transposed into political terms, but people in the nineteenth century went through torments over losing faith, lacking faith, longing for faith. I myself met, when a girl, survivors of that struggle, much battered by the experience. Now, looking back, we may hear, louder than any other voice, Matthew Arnold's "melancholy, long, withdrawing roar"—the loss of faith in God.

Levin was suicidal. In a beautifully moving chapter, Tolstoy describes his at last achieving faith: now we would say that the psychological conflict and tension were so great they would have to be resolved one way or the other.

Christianity's great contribution to human happiness has been a hatred of the body and of the flesh—distrust of women, dislike of sex. In this it is unlike the two other Middle Eastern religions. Judaism, far from denouncing sex, prescribes lovemaking for the faithful on their Sabbath, thus sanctifying and celebrating sex. Islam is not a puritan religion. Not in Judaism and Islam do we find celibate priests who use nuns or their housekeepers as their mistresses, or are driven to sex with little boys. But Christianity might have been tailored to fit Tolstoy's needs and nature.

He became what he always had the potential for—a fanatic. There are descriptions of him, after his conversion, his fevered fervid face, his bullying manner, telling people of their duty to become like him, because being a fanatic, there was only one truth, his. There is such a thing as the logic of the fanatic, who begins with a proposition or a set of them, and from there develops inexorably all the rest.

It was wrong, it was wicked, to have sex with a pregnant woman or a lactating one. His wife, Sonya, protested at his inconsistencies, but Tolstoy was never afraid of contradicting himself. Thus he is driven—by logic—at least for the period of the argument, to support polygamy, for the sensible Tolstoy knows that celibacy is impossible. He is rather like those politicians, their fiery years forgotten, who tell teenagers that it is easy to "just say no." Say no—that's all there is to it! Anyone with an ounce of common sense, or even with a working memory of their young selves, must know it is absurd: but we are in the grip of fanatic logic.

My favorite is the Inquisition, which, having burned a heretic alive, used to send their police around to collect from the relatives money to pay for the wood used for the bonfire. Who else? The relatives might not have wanted their loved one incinerated, but obviously it was they who were responsible for the monster and therefore they must pay. It makes for an entertaining, if painful, pastime, watching the logic-chopping of extremists, unfortunately so numerous in our sad times, and Tolstoy's recommendation of celibacy for the entire human race is an excellent example.

What women might think about these prohibitions (and his wife had many loudly voiced ideas of her own) did not interest Tolstoy. He insists that women are "pure." Even "as pure as doves." The sane Tolstoy knows this is rubbish, but he has to insist that women all hate sex, which is vile, shameful, and even unnatural—these are only some of his epithets. A pure maiden will always hate sex.

Chekhov, who stood by him in the fuss over the book, told him that he talked nonsense about female sexuality. At some point one does have to ask if perhaps the trouble was really a simple one: Tolstoy was no good in bed. There must be some explanation for his insistence that women dislike sex. His Sonya did not like it but saw sex as a way of keeping him at heel. When he did ask to sleep alone, she refused. She welcomed sex with him because he became friendly, simple, affectionate: if his disciples knew, she mocked, the reason for his saintliness; that his good moods were the result of sex with his wife, then they, too, would mock this apostle for total celibacy.

If Tolstoy was bad at sex, there is a parallel, D. H. Lawrence, who clearly knew little about sex: at least, the author of his earlier books did not. Yet he also wrote wonderfully about love, sexual power struggles, the higher and lower reaches of passion. Very odd, that. Later, the earthy Frieda would have taught him better, but poor Sonya Tolstoy slept with only one man in her life, whose embraces were described as bearlike.

When he is writing his great novels, there is no suggestion that his characters hate sex, but as a polemicist he says that women hate sex and after sex are cold and hostile, and that this hostility is the real relationship between men and women, concealed by the recurring cycles of sexual attraction and indifference.

When Tolstoy was very old, sex ceased, and Sonya Tolstoy complained that what she had always feared had happened: without the sexual bond all ties were cut between them. Yet, very old, they were writing loving notes saying they could not live without each other.

This cycle of sex and quarreling has always fascinated me. Anybody who has enjoyed passionate sex will recall as well passionate quarrels, but surely it is not surprising, when sex is such a promoter of strong emotions of all kinds, that antagonism should sometimes be one of them. It is not unknown, either, for people to report enjoying the crazy quarrels that may spice and heighten sex. *Enjoy*—out with the word. Woman is an unwilling victim and man the guilt-ridden and driven aggressor.

Thirteen children did his countess and Tolstoy get between them. Sonya Tolstoy had eight children in eight years. Yes, there were nannies and nursemaids, but the implications of the simple physical fact are surely enough to explain a lot of that rioting emotion.

They lost three children, in three years, to illnesses that these days would not amount to more than a few days' indisposition. Of the thirteen children they lost four. Sonya Tolstoy must always have been pregnant, nursing, and a good part of the time in mourning. Tolstoy was as affected by these deaths as his wife. After a particularly poignant death of a much-loved child, the thirteenth, he said: "Yes, he was a delightful, wonderful little boy. But what does it mean to say he is dead? There is no death; he is not dead because we love him, because he is giving us life." This apparently monstrous egotism was not what it looks like, for we have an account of Tolstoy, crazed with grief, running across the fields to escape from his emotion, repeating "in a jerky savage voice": "There is no death! There is no death!"

The Kreutzer Sonata was written after hearing the music played, which affected him strongly: he was white and suffering, and arranged to have it played again. As a result of the first hearing he made love to Sonya—if that is the word for it—and as a result of that, she got pregnant with the little boy Ivan, who died seven years later and caused Tolstoy to insist: There is no death.

By this time he was claiming that there was no justification for art that is not polemical. In 1865 he wrote, "The aims of art are incommensurable with the aims of socialism. An artist's mission must not be to produce an irrefutable solution to a problem, but to compel us to love life in all its countless and inexhaustible manifestations." By the time he was writing socialist and religious tracts, art nevertheless sometimes triumphed over polemics, in *Resurrection,* for instance, in *The Death of Ivan Ilyich.*

Not very long after this tract against sex, *The Kreutzer Sonata,* which no one could say is not a compelling read, came Bohemianism, to be intensified by the First World War and its social aftermath, Free Love and "live, drink and be merry for tomorrow we die." As early as 1907 there was a scene like a rude riposte to Tolstoy and his *Kreutzer Sonata:* Ida John dying in Paris of puerperal fever, lifting her glass in a toast of champagne "to love" with her rapscallion of a husband, Augustus John, then at the height of his fame. In the next room his mistress is looking after the children.

The Bohemians, who repudiated all conventional sexual morality as thoroughly as did Tolstoy, though from the opposite viewpoint, were then a minority which set out to shock. Épatering the bourgeoisie was their raison d'être. And then, not so long after that, came the Second World War, and wartime morality, and then what a witty friend used to call "the horizontal handshake," and now young women depart from all over Europe in droves for holiday shores where they screw, presumably enjoyably, with males who wait for them like Inuits for migrating moose.

Hedonism rules, okay?

What has happened? Birth control has.

In *Anna Karenina,* Dolly, overburdened with children, visits bad Anna the outcast from society, who confides that she knows how to prevent conception. Anna is kind enough not to point out that she is still young and pretty while Dolly is worn out with childbearing. Shock and horror is what Dolly feels. She is repulsed. And that is what Tolstoy feels about birth control. It is unnatural, says he, and women make monsters of themselves, destroying in themselves their capacity for being women, that is, mothers, so that "men may have no interruption of their enjoyment." Note that it is the men who are doing the enjoying.

Anna Karenina is always talked of as the story of Anna, a society beauty, and her seducer, Vronsky, a variation of the great nineteenth-century theme of adultery. Its fame as the greatest of the adultery novels (some claim that for *Madame Bovary*) tends to obscure the scope of the novel: Tolstoy portrayed a gallery of women of that time. Dolly is the unhappy wife of a bad husband. Kitty is the happy wife of a jealous and loving husband. There are court ladies, whom Tolstoy detests, and peasant women, whom he admires. One is Levin's housekeeper, more of a friend than a servant, and the peasant woman who came to rescue Dolly from her domestic disorders. A young peasant woman shocked Dolly by saying that "the Lord has relieved me of a burden," talking of the death of a child—one mouth less to feed. A spinster fails to get a husband and is doomed to a life of being a guest in other people's houses. A bad woman—Anna Karenina's mirror—is a prostitute and can have no future. This is a novel about the situation of women in that time. Anna now would not have to throw herself under a train. Dolly would not have so many children. Kitty perhaps would not be so content as the wife of an unreasonably jealous man. The spinster would have a career, might be a single mother. Nowhere in *Anna Karenina* does that great artist describe a wife or mistress disgusted with sex and full of implacable hatred for men's sexuality. Anna hates Vronsky at the end because he is free and she is not, but she does not hate him sexually.

There is just a hint of the conflict between the moralist and the artist in this novel, which begins with the inscription, like a curse, "Vengeance is mine, I will repay" saith the Lord. But there is no vengeance; the novel is irradiated by Tolstoy's love and understanding of everything.

Understanding of everything and everybody but not of himself. He said to Gorky, "Man can endure earthquake, epidemics, dreadful diseases, every form of spiritual torment, but the most dreadful tragedy that can befall him and will remain, is the tragedy of the bedroom."

We have the diaries of two people with a gift for complaint, invective, and a relish for recording the minutiae of the ups and downs of their love. For it was that. In between the storms were days of tranquillity. We have all the facts, or think we have, but few of us now have the experiences that could tell us what life in that family was like.

Yasnaya Polyana—which can translate as Aspen Glades, or Bright

Glades—the Tolstoys' country house, is now a shrine, and visited by thousands every year. It was the estate's manor house, a large villa with many rooms that turned out not to be enough to accommodate all those children, and so a wing was built on. There were all kinds of sheds, huts, and annexes. Now it has to impress us by its potentialities for discomfort, because of the numbers of people it had to house. Large, high-ceilinged rooms, which must have been hell to heat. In summer, set as it is in fields and woods, what a paradise—but there is a long Russian winter. The furniture is adequate. The sofa where Tolstoy was born and where the countess labored thirteen times is hard, slippery, ungiving.

Fresh water did not come gushing from taps: it was brought in by the bucket and there was a bathhouse. No electric light. There is a scene of Tolstoy, an old man, writing in his study with the aid of a single candle.

The house held the parents, thirteen children, servants, nursemaids, tutors—one lived there with his wife and two children—governesses, relatives, and many visitors. There were also the disciples, who expected to be fed and, often, housed, sometimes for weeks. They would fit themselves into the servants' rooms in the attic—what happened to them?—or bed down in the corridors. It was usual to have thirty people sit down for a meal. Comfort of the sort we take for granted, there was none. Privacy, which we have learned to need, was not easily got. Tolstoy had his study, but it was permeable by anyone who decided he or she had the right—Sonya, and his chief disciple, the appalling Chertkov, and people demanding spiritual counseling. Once out of his study, then he was part of everything. The quarrels of adults, the squabbles of children, the crying of babies, the arguments of the disciples must have reverberated in those wooden walls. The countess understandably complained of "nerves," and surely Tolstoy was entitled to them too.

Thirteen children. Thirteen. *Thirteen.* Four, dead. We are not talking about a peasant woman, a farm woman, with expectations for a hard life, but an educated sensitive woman who could never have dreamed of the kind of life she in fact had to lead.

There is a tirade in *The Kreutzer Sonata* about the unhappiness that children bring, mostly the misery of the fear of their dying: the slightest indisposition could become a serious illness. In both *Anna Karenina* and *War and Peace* the difficulties of childbearing and child-rearing are depicted. Tolstoy was not a father removed from the burdens of the family. How could he have been, in that house? He knew all about pregnancy and morning sickness, and milk fever and cracked nipples. He knew about the discomforts of breast-feeding and sleepless nights. His great novels accepted life's ills, as they accepted its delights; everything is in balance, in proportion; but somewhere, at some point, it became impossible for him to stand his life. A skin had been ripped off him: it must have happened. It is often enough suggested that Sonya Tolstoy was a bit demented; we must remember that she copied out *War and Peace* and all the other novels, many times, while she was carrying and giving birth and nursing and serving her Leo, who, she complained, insisted on his marital rights before she was even healed after childbirth. Surely Leo Tolstoy became a bit demented too, quite apart from the old man's infatuation with his disciple Chertkov, who was like a horrible caricature of himself.

Those of us who have known people with clinical depression, or suffering the dark night of the soul, have heard descriptions of spiritual landscapes so dreadful that attempts at consolation ring as false as badly tuned pianos. And so they are received by the sufferers, who look at you with a contempt for your superficiality. "What I am feeling now, that's the truth," they may actually spell out to the stupid one. "When you are depressed you see the truth; the rest is illusion." So one feels reading *The Kreutzer Sonata*. Here is a landscape of despair—no exit! Remember the cage he had made for himself, this highly sexed man. Sex—bad. Sex with a pregnant or nursing woman—bad. No sex outside marriage. A recipe for guilt and self-hatred. The wasteland he describes that lacks any joy, pleasure—one hardly dare use the word love—is the truth. So be it.

Let us imagine ourselves back in that house. It is night, supper over, the visitors and disciples in their nooks and corners. The older children are still up, studying or playing, and their voices are loud and so are their feet on the wooden floors. The little ones are in their rooms with their nurses and are as noisy as small children are.

Tolstoy wants to be a husband tonight—so he puts it. God is not coming to his aid in his battles with lust.

Sonya's newest baby is six months old. She is afraid that she is pregnant again. She has to be in a state of conflict as her Leo approaches, smiling and affectionate: carefree sex has not yet been invented in the world's laboratories. She has never known it, never, in her long married life. If not pregnant already, then she may become so tonight. The count and countess, Leo and Sonya, make sure the doors are shut, and hope the children won't come up wanting something. The new baby is in the next room with his nurse. He is hungry and can be heard grizzling. Leo must be careful not to touch Sonya's breasts, which are swollen with milk. She tried hard at first to refuse breast-feeding, and use wet nurses, because her nipples always crack, and nursing is a torture, but Leo insisted on her breast-feeding. And he must remember that her cracked nipples sometimes bleed, if he is impatient or clumsy. The baby is really going at it now: his hungry howls will bring the nursemaid in with him if she and Leo can't get a move on. The nursemaid, a girl from the village, is singing a peasant lullaby, and the sound and the rhythms become part of Leo's thrusting, which in any case has extra vigor because he rather fancies the girl. "Oh, God," thinks Sonya, "please don't let me get pregnant. Oh, I do hope I'm not pregnant, my poor nipples will never get a chance to heal." In spite of her care, trying to shield her breasts with her hands, milk suddenly spurts all over the bed, herself, his hands. She is weeping with self-disgust and discomfort but quite pleased she has this excuse to make Leo feel the greedy beast he is. The sheets will need washing: they were put on clean that morning. The girl who does the washing will complain again: too much washing with all these people as well as the children and it is so hard to get things dry, when the weather is bad, as it is now. Sonya's weeping infuriates Leo, and he is full of guilt and self-dislike. She is thinking that all this milk is being wasted, though she is trying to stop it flowing, while the baby's yelling from next door is making it flow. The baby, who is now screaming, is a big feeder and not easily satisfied. "I'll have to heat up a little milk for him," she is thinking. "I hope the children didn't finish it all at supper. They never bring up enough milk for the house—how am I to manage with all these people?" She tells Leo to get right out of bed and leave her in peace to clean up. Yes, he can come back later, if he likes, when she's fed the baby. He says he'll sleep in his study tonight. "Yes," she thinks, "you've got what you wanted and now you can forget me." She feels abandoned and punished.

He goes off, praying that God will answer his prayers and damp down his lusts.

This scene, or something like it, must have happened a hundred times.

No wonder prostitutes were popular, to take the strain off such marriage beds: Leo himself said this once, but now he has changed his mind and says that prostitution is wicked. Why should poor innocent women be degraded by the filthy lusts of men?

To read this book now is like listening to a scream of anguish from a hell that women have escaped from, and men, too. But wait a minute: it is in what we call the West that people have escaped, or most of us. When we read that a woman in Africa, or India, or anywhere in the poor countries of the world has had eight children, and three died, then the world of Yasnaya Polyana and *The Kreutzer Sonata* isn't so far away.

———

DORIS LESSING is one of the most celebrated and distinguished writers of the second half of the twentieth century. Her most recent books include the novels *The Sweetest Dream, Mara and Dann,* and *Ben, in the World,* and the two volumes of autobiography, *Under My Skin* and *Walking in the Shade.* She lives in north London.

But I say unto you, That whosoever looketh on a woman to lust after her hath committed adultery with her already in his heart.

MATT. 5:28.

His disciples say unto him, If the case of the man be so with his wife, it is not good to marry. But he said unto them, All men cannot receive this saying, save they to whom it is given.

MATT. 19:10–11.

THE
KREUTZER
SONATA

CHAPTER I

It was early spring. We had been traveling for more than twenty-four hours. Passengers with tickets for various places along the way had been boarding and leaving our carriage, but there were four of us who had been on the train from the very start—a weary-faced lady, neither beautiful nor young, wearing a hat and mannish overcoat, who smoked cigarettes; her companion, a talkative man of forty, with neat new luggage; and thirdly, a rather short and very reserved gentleman with prematurely gray curly hair, with very nervous mannerisms, and with extraordinarily brilliant eyes which kept roving from object to object. He wore an old overcoat with a lamb's-wool collar, quite obviously made by an expensive tailor, and a high lamb's-wool hat. Under his overcoat, when it was thrown open, were visible a sleeveless kaftan[1] and an embroidered Russian shirt. He had a peculiar habit: from time to time he produced strange noises like a cough or like a laugh begun and suddenly broken off. During the whole journey, he carefully avoided all acquaintance and conversation with the other passengers. If anyone spoke to him, he replied briefly and stiffly; for the most part he either read, smoked, gazed out the window, ate some food he took out of his old bag, and drank tea.

It seemed to me that he was oppressed by his loneliness, and several times I was tempted to speak with him, but whenever our eyes met—as often happened, since we sat diagonally opposite each other—he turned back to his book or looked out of the window.

Just before the evening of our second day, during a stop at a large station, this nervous gentleman left the carriage to get some hot water with which to make himself some tea. The gentleman with the neat new luggage—a lawyer, I afterward learned—went out with the cigarette-smoking lady in the mannish overcoat to drink tea in the station. During their absence, several new persons entered our carriage, among them a tall, closely shaven, wrinkled old man, evidently a merchant, wearing a coat of polecat fur and a cloth cap with a huge vizor. He sat down opposite the lawyer's seat and immediately entered into conversation with a young man, apparently a merchant's clerk, who entered the carriage at the same station.

I was sitting diagonally opposite, and since the train was stationary and no one was passing between us, I could hear snatches of their conversation.

The merchant first mentioned that he was on his way to his estate, which was situated only one station distant. Then, as usual, they began to talk about prices, about trade, and about the current state of business in Moscow. After that, their conversation turned to the Fair at Nizhni-Novgorod.

The clerk began to tell about the merrymaking of a rich merchant whom both of them knew at the Fair, but the old man interrupted to tell about the merrymakings which had taken place in former times at Kunavin and which he himself had enjoyed. He was evidently proud of the share he had taken in them, for with manifest delight he related how he and this same common acquaintance had once got drunk at Kunavin and played such tricks that he had to tell about them in a whisper. The clerk burst out in hearty laughter which filled the whole carriage, and the old man laughed too, revealing two yellow teeth.

Not expecting to hear anything interesting, I got up to go out on the platform till the train should start. At the door I met the lawyer and the lady, talking in a very animated manner as they walked.

"You won't have much time," said the sociable lawyer. "The second bell will ring in a moment."

And, in fact, I did not even have time to walk to the end of the carriage before the bell rang. When I got back to my place the lively conversation between the lawyer and the lady was still going on. The old merchant sat facing them silently and sternly, occasionally showing his disapproval by chewing on his teeth.

". . . whereupon she explained to her husband bluntly," the lawyer was saying with a smile as I passed them, "that she could not and, moreover, would not, live with him, since . . ."

And he proceeded to tell something more which I could not hear. Behind me came other passengers, then came the conductor, followed by a porter bustling through, and there was so much noise for a time that I could not hear what they were talking about.

When it grew quieter the lawyer's voice was heard again, but the conversation had evidently gone over from a particular instance to general considerations. The lawyer was saying that the question of divorce was now occupying general attention in Europe and that the phenomenon was appearing more and more frequently in Russia.

Noticing that his voice alone was heard, the lawyer cut his words short and turned to the old man.

"It wasn't so in old times, was it?" he remarked, smiling pleasantly.

The old man was about to make some answer, but just then the train started, and, taking off his cap, he crossed himself and began to whisper a prayer. The lawyer, turning his eyes away, waited politely. Having finished his prayer and crossed himself three times, the old man put on his cap and pulled it down, and began to speak.

"The same thing took place, sir, in old times, only less frequently," said he. "At the present time it can't help happening. People have grown cultured!"

The train, moving along more and more rapidly, thundered so loudly I could hardly hear. But since the discussion interested me, I moved to a nearer seat. My neighbor, the nervous bright-eyed gentleman, was also evidently much interested, and he listened, but without moving from his place.

"In what respect are we ill-educated?" asked the lady, with a scarcely perceptible smile. "Do you mean that it would be better for men and women to get married as they used to in old times, when the bride and bridegroom never even saw each other before the wedding?"

She went on, replying, after the fashion of many women, not to her neighbor's words but to the words she thought he would say. "People didn't know whether they would love each other or not. They just married whoever fell to their lot, and often they were miserable their whole lives long! So you think that our old way was the best, do you?" she continued, addressing her remarks mainly to me and the lawyer, and least of all to the old man with whom she was talking.

"We have already become very cultured," repeated the merchant, looking scornfully at the lady and leaving her question unanswered.

"I should like to know how you explain the connection between culture and matrimonial quarrels," said the lawyer with a slight smile.

The merchant was about to say something but the lady interrupted him.

"No, those days are gone," she said. But the lawyer interrupted her.

"Let him say what he thinks."

"The nonsense of culture!" said the old man resolutely.

"People who do not love each other marry and then wonder that they don't get along," said the lady hastily, glancing at the lawyer and then at me and even at the clerk, who had got up and, standing with his elbow on the back of the chair, was listening to the conversation with a smile. "Animals can be paired off in this way as their master may wish, but men and women have individual preferences and attachments," she said, evidently wanting to say something severe to the old merchant.

"When you speak this way, madame," said the old man, "you are wrong. Animals are brutes, but man has a law."

"But how can one live with a man when there is no love?" insisted the lady, eager to express an opinion which apparently seemed to her very novel.

"In former times they did not discuss this," said the old man in a magisterial tone. "It is only a recent development. For the least reason the wife cries out, 'I will leave you.' Even among the peasants this new behavior has come into fashion. 'Here,' says the peasant's wife, 'here are your shirts and drawers, but I am going off with Vanka; his hair is curlier than yours.' Reasoning is no help. For a woman the first thing needed is fear."

The clerk, suppressing a smile, looked at the lawyer and at the lady and at me, ready either to laugh at or to approve the merchant's argument according to the way the others received it.

"Fear of what?" asked the lady.

"Why, fear of her husband of course—that kind of fear."

"But, my dear sir, the day for that sort of thing has long passed," said the lady with no little sharpness.

"No, madame, the time for that can never be passed. Eve was created out of man's rib, and so it will remain till the end of time," said the old man, nodding his head so sternly and triumphantly that the clerk instantly decided that the victory was on the merchant's side and he burst out into loud laughter.

"Yes, that is the way you men decide," said the lady, not yielding and looking at us. "You give yourselves full liberty but you want to keep the women locked up. For you, of course, all things are permitted."

"It is not a matter of permission. The fact is that man is not the childbearer in the family; it is the woman who is the fragile vessel," suggested the merchant. The positiveness of the merchant's tone evidently impressed his hearers, and even the lady felt crushed but still she would not give in.

"Yes, but I think you will agree that a woman is a human being and has feelings as well as a man. Well, then, what is she going to do if she does not love her husband?"

"Not love her husband?" exclaimed the merchant in a savage tone, making a grimace with his lips and his eyebrows. "Don't worry, she'll come to love him." This unexpected argument especially pleased the clerk, who grunted his agreement.

"But that is not so. She may not come to love him," insisted the lady. "And if there is no love, then they ought not to be compelled to continue."

"But if a woman is false to her husband, what then?" asked the lawyer.

"That is not to be supposed," said the old man. "He must make sure that doesn't happen."

"But if it does happen, what then? It has happened . . ."

"Yes, there are cases, but not among us," said the old man.

All were silent. The clerk leaned forward a little more, and not wishing to be left out of the conversation, began with a smile. "Well, there was a scandal in the home of a fine young fellow in our company. It was very hard to decide about it. The woman was very fond of amusements, and she began to play the devil; but her husband was a reasonable and cultured man. At first she flirted with one of the clerks. Her husband argued kindly with her, but she would not stop. She did all sorts of underhanded things and even stole her husband's money. He flogged her, but it did no good. She only acted worse. Then she had an affair with an unchristened Jew. What could he do? He turned her out, and now he lives like a bachelor and she is a woman-about-town."

"That's because he was a fool," said the old man. "If at the very beginning he had not given her her head, but had given her a good sound scolding, she would have been all right, I tell you! A woman must not have her own way at first. Don't trust a horse in the field or your wife in your house."

At this moment the conductor came along to take up the tickets for the next station, and the old man gave him his.

"Yes," said he, "we've got to restrain the female sex or else everything will go to ruin."

"But you were just telling how you married men enjoyed yourselves at the Fair at Kunavin," said I, unable to restrain myself.

"That was a personal matter," said the merchant, and he lapsed into silence.

When the whistle sounded, the merchant got up, took his bag from under the seat, put on his coat, and, lifting his cap, went out to the platform.

CHAPTER II

As soon as the old man had gone out, several people spoke up at once.

"An Old Testament patriarch!" exclaimed the clerk.

"The *Domostroy*[2] come to life!" said the lady. "What savage notions of women and marriage!"

"Yes, indeed, we are still far from the European view of marriage," said the lawyer.

"The thing these men simply cannot understand," said the lady, "is that marriage without love just is not marriage, that love alone consecrates marriage, and that the only true marriage is that which love consecrates."

The clerk listened and smiled, trying to remember for future use as much as he could of the clever conversation.

In the midst of the lady's sentence, we heard a sound just behind me like an interrupted laugh or a sob, and looking around we saw my neighbor—the bright-eyed, gray-haired, solitary gentleman—who during the conversation, which had evidently interested him, had unobtrusively moved near. He was standing with his hand resting on the back of the seat. He was clearly very agitated; his face was red and the muscles of his cheek twitched.

"What is that love . . . that love . . . which consecrates marriage?" he asked, stammering.

The lady, seeing his agitated state, tried to answer him as gently and fully as possible.

"True love. It is true love between a man and a woman which makes marriage possible," said the lady.

"Yes, but what do you mean by true love?" asked the gentleman, smiling awkwardly and timidly.

"Everyone knows what true love is," she replied, wishing to cut short her conversation with him.

"But I for one don't," said the gentleman. "You must define what you mean by it."

"Why, it's very simple," said the lady, but she hesitated. "Love . . . love is the . . . is the exclusive preference which a man or woman feels for one person out of all the rest in the world."

"A preference for how long a time? A month? Two months? Half an hour?" asked the gray-haired man and laughed.

"No, but—excuse me, you are evidently not talking about the same thing."

"Yes, I am talking about the same thing."

"She says," interrupted the lawyer, indicating the lady, "that marriage ought to result in the first place from an attachment—from love, if you will—and that when such a love actually exists, only marriage furnishes, so to speak, some consecration. Therefore, any marriage in which there is no genuine attachment as a foundation—love, if you wish to call it that—has no moral obligation. Do I express your idea correctly?" he asked, addressing the lady.

She nodded her head in agreement with his interpretation.

"Therefore . . ." the lawyer continued.

But the nervous gentleman, his eyes agleam and restraining himself with difficulty, began, without allowing the lawyer to proceed, "No, I am speaking about the same thing, about the preference that one man or one woman has for one person above all others. I simply ask how long this preference is to last?"

"How long? Why, sometimes it lasts a whole lifetime," said the lady, shrugging her shoulders.

"Yes, but that is true only in novels, never in real life. In real life this preference for one person may occasionally last a year, but more often it is measured by months, or even by weeks or days or hours," he said, evidently realizing with some satisfaction that he was surprising everyone by his opinion.

"Oh, what are you saying?" . . . "No, excuse me!" . . . "Oh, no!" three of us broke in with one voice, and even the clerk uttered a disapproving grunt.

"Yes, I know," interrupted the gray-haired gentleman. "You are speaking of what does not exist. Every man feels for every pretty woman what you call love."

"Oh, what you say is awful! Surely there exists among human beings that feeling which is called love and which lasts not merely for months and years, but for whole lives!"

"No, I don't agree. Even if it is granted that a man may keep his preference for a given woman all his life, the woman in all probability will prefer someone else, and so it has always been in the world and always will be," he said, and, taking out a cigarette, he began to smoke.

"But it may be reciprocal," said the lawyer.

"No, that is impossible," he insisted, "just as impossible as that in a load of peas there should be two peas exactly alike, side by side. And over and above this improbability there is also the likelihood of satiety. That one will love the same person a whole life long is like expecting that a single candle will burn forever," he said, inhaling the smoke of his cigarette deeply.

"But you are talking about physical love. Don't you admit that there is a love based on a unity of ideals, on a spiritual affinity?" asked the lady.

"Spiritual affinity! Unity of ideals!" he repeated, emitting his peculiar sound. "In that case there is no reason why we should sleep together—excuse my bluntness. Is it because of this unity of ideals that people go to bed together?" he asked, laughing nervously.

"But, pardon me," said the lawyer, "what you say is contradicted by the facts. We see that marriage exists, that all the human race—or the majority of it—lives a married life, and many live honorably all their days in this marriage relation."

The gray-haired gentleman laughed again.

"You were just saying that marriage is founded on love, but when I said I doubted the existence of any love except the sentimental kind, you then tried to prove the existence of love by the fact that marriages exist. But marriages in these days are all falsehood."

"Oh, no, excuse me," exclaimed the lawyer. "I only say that marriages have always existed and still exist."

"Yes, but *why* do they exist? They have existed and still exist for people who see in marriage something sacred, a sacrament which is entered into before God. For such people it exists. Among us, people get married, seeing nothing in marriage except copulation, and the result is either deception or violence. When it is deception, it is easier to endure. Husband and wife only deceive people into believing that they are living a monogamous marriage, but they are really practicing polygamy. It is bad, but still it is the general custom. But when, as happens oftener, people take on an external obligation to live together all their lives—and even from the second month they hate each other and want to separate, and yet they go on living together—then follows that terrible hell from which they try to escape by drinking, by duels, by killing and poisoning themselves and others," he went on, talking more and more rapidly and growing more and more excited. It became embarrassing for all of us.

"Yes, without doubt there are critical episodes in married life," said the lawyer, trying to cut short this unseemly and heated conversation.

"I imagine you have guessed who I am," the gray-haired gentleman said, softly and with a certain appearance of calm.

"No, I have not that pleasure."

"The pleasure will not be great. My name is Pozdnyshev, the man in whose life happened that critical episode to which you referred— the episode of a man killing his wife," he said, glancing swiftly at each one of us.

No one knew what to say. We all remained silent.

"Well, it is no matter," he said, with a grunt. "Excuse me. I will not trouble you any more."

"Not at all," said the lawyer, himself not knowing exactly what he meant.

But Pozdnyshev, not heeding him, turned quickly and went back to his seat. The lawyer talked in whispers with the lady. I sat down next to Pozdnyshev and, unable to think of anything to say, said nothing. It was now too dark to read, so I shut my eyes and pretended that I was going to sleep.

We rode in silence this way till we reached the next station. There, the lawyer and lady were transferred to another carriage, something they had arranged beforehand with the conductor. The clerk got into a comfortable position on his sofa and went to sleep. Pozdnyshev kept smoking, and drank some tea which he had got at the station.

When I opened my eyes and looked at him, he suddenly turned to me with an expression of resolution and exasperation.

"Maybe it is disagreeable for you to be sitting with me, now that you know who I am. If that is so, I will move."

"Oh, not at all . . . please."

"Well, then, wouldn't you like some tea? Only it's rather strong."

He poured me some tea.

"They say—but then they all lie . . ." he said.

"What are you speaking about?" I asked.

"Always about the same thing—about love and what people mean by it. Don't you prefer to sleep?"

"Not at all."

"Then, if you would like me to, I will tell you how I was led by this very same kind of love to do what I did."

"I certainly would, unless it would be painful for you."

"No, I would like to talk about it. Drink your tea—or is it too strong?"

The tea was really like dark beer, but I drank a glass of it. At this moment the conductor came along. Pozdnyshev silently watched him with angry eyes, and did not begin until he had left the car.

CHAPTER III

"Well, then, I will tell you. But are you sure you would like to have me do so?"

I assured him that I was very eager to hear him. He remained silent a little while, rubbed his face with his hands, and began.

"If I tell you, I must begin at the very beginning. I must tell you how and why I got married, and what I was before I married.

"Up to the time of my marriage I lived as all men live; that is, all the men in my circle. I am a landowner and a university graduate, and I have presided at the District Council as a marshal of the nobility.[3] Up to the time of my marriage I lived, as all men live, a dissipated life; and, like all the young men of our circle, though living a dissipated life, I was convinced that I was living as I ought. Regarding myself, I thought I was a charming person and a perfectly moral man. I was no vulgar seducer and I had no unnatural tastes; I did not make this sort of thing my chief object in life, as did many of my intimates; I indulged in dissipation moderately and decently for my health's sake; I avoided such women as might, by the birth of a child or by the force of attachment to me, entangle me. There may, of course, have been children and there may have been attachments, but I acted as if there was nothing of the sort. I not only considered this sort of behavior moral, but I was proud of it."

He paused, emitting his peculiar sound, as he apparently always did when a new thought occurred to him.

"And precisely here is the chief viciousness of it all!" he said vigorously. "Depravity does not lie in anything physical; it does not imply any physical abnormality. Depravity—genuine depravity—consists in freeing oneself from moral relations with women with whom you enter into physical relations. And this emancipation I considered a virtue. I remember how much it bothered me that one time I had not paid a woman who apparently loved me and had given herself to me, and I was only content again when I sent her the money—to show her that I did not consider myself morally bound to her. Don't shake your head as if you agreed with me!" he suddenly cried. "I know that you too, unless you are a rare exception, have just such views as I had then. Well, no matter, please excuse me," he went on. "But this is the whole trouble and it is awful! awful! awful!"

"What is awful?" I asked.

"The abyss of error in which we live concerning women and our relations to them. I cannot talk with calm about it, and the reason I cannot is the episode which took place in my life. But ever since that occurred, my eyes have been opened, and I have seen everything in an entirely different light—exactly the opposite . . . exactly the opposite."

He smoked his cigarette, and, leaning his elbows on his knees, went on talking. In the darkness I could not see his face very clearly, but above the rattle and rumble of the train I could hear his strong and pleasant voice.

CHAPTER IV

"Yes, only by tormenting myself as I have, only so have I learned where the root of the whole trouble is. I have learned what must be, and therefore have come to see the whole horror of what is.

"Now you will see how and when things happened which led to

that episode I mentioned. It began when I was not quite sixteen years old. I was still in high school and my oldest brother was a student at the university. I had not known a woman yet at that time but, like all the unfortunate boys of our circle, I was by no means an innocent child. Two years before I had been corrupted by coarse boys. Already woman, not any particular woman, but woman as a sweet something, woman, any woman—woman in her nakedness—had already begun to torment me. My solitudes were unchaste. I was tormented as ninety-nine per cent of our boys are tormented. I was afraid, I struggled, I prayed, and—I fell! My imagination was already corrupt. I myself was corrupt but the final step had not yet been taken. I was ruined by myself even before I had put my hands on another human being. But here a friend of my brother's, a gay young student, a so-called good fellow—in other words, the greatest good-for-nothing possible, who had already taught us to drink and to play cards—persuaded us after a drinking session to go *there*.

"We went. My brother had also been innocent, and he fell the same night. And I, a boy of fifteen, debased myself and accomplished the debasement of a woman, not at all understanding the enormity of what I was doing. You see, I had never learned from any of my elders that what I was doing was wrong. And even now no one ever says so. To be sure it is contained in the Ten Commandments, but the Commandments seem to be known only in order to pass an examination by a priest, and even then are not regarded as very important—not nearly so important as the rule for the use of *ut* in conditional sentences!

"Thus I had never heard a single one of my elders, whom I respected, say that what we did was wrong. On the contrary, I heard men whom I respected say it was a good thing. I heard them say that one's struggles and sufferings were relieved after that. I heard it and I read it, and I heard my elders say that it was good for the health. From my friends I heard that there was merit, even gallantry, in such conduct. So there was nothing to be expected from it but beneficial effects. Danger of disease? Even that is taken care of. A solicitous government looks out for that. It looks after and regulates the activity of brothels and makes lewdness safe. And doctors for a consideration do the same. Thus it comes about: they affirm that lewdness is good for the health and they make a regular institution of lewdness. I know of mothers who see to it that their sons' health is cared for in this way. And science follows them into the brothels."

"Why science?" I asked.

"What are doctors? The priests of science. Who corrupts young men by declaring that this is necessary for the health? They do.

"It is certain that if one per cent of the energy employed in the cure of syphilis were expended in the eradication of lewdness, syphilis would long ago have become a memory. But instead the energy is expended, not in the eradication of lewdness, but in guaranteeing the safety of lewdness. Well, that is not the trouble. The trouble consists in this, that with me, as with nine out of ten, if not even more—not only of our class, but of all, even the peasantry—the horrible fact is that I fell, not by yielding to a single temptation of the charm of any special woman—no, no special woman led me astray—I fell because those around me saw in what was really a fall either a lawful act, a desirable regulator for the health, or a natural and simple, even innocent, diversion for a young man.

"I did not even realize that this was a fall. I simply began to give myself up to those pleasures, to those necessities, which, as it was suggested to me, were natural—gave myself up to this dissipation in the same way that I had begun to drink and smoke. And yet there was something unusual and pathetic in this first fall. I remember well how immediately—even before I left that room—a feeling of sadness, deep sadness, came over me, so that I felt like weeping, weeping for the loss of my innocence, for a forever sullied relationship to womanhood. Yes, the natural, simple relationship I had enjoyed with women was now forever impossible. Purity of relationship with any woman was at an end; it could never be again. I had become what is called a libertine. And to be a libertine is to be in a physical condition like that of a drug addict, a drunkard, or a smoker. As any one of these is no longer a normal man, so a man who uses women for his own pleasure is no longer normal; he is a man forever spoiled—a libertine. As the drunkard or the addict can be instantly recognized by his face, by his actions, so it is with the rake. He may restrain himself, may struggle with his inclinations, but his simple, pure, sincere, and fraternal relations with woman are no longer possible. By the very way in which he looks at a young woman, or stares at her, the libertine is recognized. So I became a libertine, and I remained one, and that was my ruin.

CHAPTER V

"Yes, so it was. So it went on and on, and every kind of depravity ensued. My God! When I remember all my abominable actions I am overwhelmed with horror. I remember how my friends used to laugh at my so-called innocence. And when you hear about the gilded youth, the officers, the young Parisians!

"And all these gentlemen, and I, when we—libertines of thirty, having on our souls hundreds of the most varied and horrible crimes against woman—when we come into the drawing room or the ballroom, freshly washed, cleanly shaven, well perfumed, in immaculate linen, in evening dress or uniform—what emblems of purity! how charming we are!

"Just think what ought to be and what is! It ought to be that when such a gentleman comes into the society of my sister or my daughter, I, knowing about his life, should draw him quietly to one side and say in a confidential whisper, 'I know exactly how you are living, how you spend your nights and with whom. This is no place for you. These are pure, innocent women and girls. Please go.'

"So it ought to be. But in reality, when such a man makes his appearance or when he dances with my sister or my daughter in his arms, we rejoice if he is rich and well connected. Perhaps he will honor my daughter after Rigolboche.[4] Even if traces of his disease remain, it is of no consequence; the cure is easy nowadays. I know that some girls of the highest society have been given by their parents with enthusiasm to men who have certain diseases. Oh, what rottenness! But the time is coming when this rottenness and falsehood will be ended."

Several times he emitted his strange noises and sipped his tea. His tea was terribly strong, and there was no water at hand to weaken it. I was aware that the two glasses I had drunk had greatly affected my nerves. The tea must have had a great effect on him also because he kept growing more and more excited. His voice kept growing louder and more emphatic. He kept changing his position; one moment he would remove his hat, then he would put it on again; and his face kept changing strangely in the twilight in which we were sitting.

"Well, that was the way I lived until I was thirty years of age, never for a moment abandoning my intention of getting married and enjoying the most lofty and unsullied existence. And with this end in mind I looked at every girl," he continued. "I was soiled with lewdness and yet, at the same time, I was looking for a girl whose purity would meet my standards. I rejected many of them instantly on the ground that they were not sufficiently pure for me, but at last I found one whom I thought worthy of me. She was one of the two daughters of a man in Penza, who had formerly been very rich but was now quite poor. One evening, after we had been out in a boat and were returning home by moonlight, I was sitting alongside her and admiring her well-proportioned figure clad in a jersey, and her attractive curls, when suddenly I made up my mind that *she* was the one. It seemed to me that evening that she understood everything I felt and thought, and I had the most elevated thoughts. In reality it was simply that her jersey was especially becoming to her, and so were her curls, and that, having spent a day in her immediate presence, I wanted to be even closer to her.

"It is a remarkable thing how full of illusion is the notion that beauty is an advantage. A beautiful woman says all sorts of foolishness; you listen and do not hear any foolishness—what you hear seems to you wisdom itself. She says and does common things; to you it seems lovely. Even when she does not say stupid or common things but is simply beautiful, you are convinced that she is miraculously wise and moral.

"I returned home enraptured and certain that she was high above others in moral perfection and therefore fit to be my wife. The next day I proposed.

"See what an entanglement it was! Out of a thousand married men—not only in our rank, but unfortunately also in the masses—there is scarcely one who, like Don Juan, would not have been married already not merely ten times, but even a hundred or a thousand times before the marriage ceremony.

"It is true there are now—so I hear, and I believe it—some young men who live pure lives, feeling and knowing that this is no joke, but a serious matter.

"God help them! But in my time there was not one such out of ten thousand. And all men know this and pretend that they do not know it.

In novels the feelings of the heroes, the ponds, the bushes around which they wander, are described in detail; but though their overpowering love for some particular maiden is described, nothing is said about what the interesting hero was doing before, not a word about his frequenting brothels, about his relations with chambermaids, cooks, and other women. Novels of this improper kind—if there are any—are not put into the hands of those who most need to know about these things—that is, young women.

"At first they pretend to young women that this dissipation, which fills half the life of our cities and villages, does not exist at all.

"In time, we ourselves become so accustomed to this hypocrisy that we actually come to believe that all of us really are moral men and live in a moral world! Girls, poor things, believe this with seriousness!

"So did my wife believe too. I remember how, after we became engaged, I showed her my diary[5] so that she might learn as much as she would like, even though it were very little, of my past and especially about the last affair in which I had been involved, for she might later hear about this from others and I felt it better to tell her. I remember her horror, her despair and disillusionment when she knew it all and realized what it meant. I saw that she was tempted to break our engagement. And why didn't she do it?"

He emitted his peculiar sound, took another swallow of tea, and paused before resuming.

CHAPTER VI

"No, on the whole it is much better, ever so much better so," he went on. "I deserved it. But that is not the point. I mean that in this business the only persons deceived are the poor unfortunate girls.

"Their mothers certainly know all this as well as anyone because they have been told by their husbands. And yet they pretend they believe in the purity of men though in reality they do not. They know by what bait to catch men for themselves and for their daughters. And we men don't know—we don't know because we don't want to know—but women know perfectly well that the loftiest and most poetic love depends not on moral qualities but on physical closeness and on the way of doing up one's hair, one's complexion, the cut of a gown. Ask an experienced coquette which she would prefer to risk: being detected in falsehood, cruelty, even immorality, in the presence of the one she is trying to entice, or to appear before him in a badly made or unbecoming gown—and she will always choose the first. She knows that man lies when he talks about lofty feelings—all he wants is the body—and so he pardons anything but an ugly, unbecoming, unfashionable costume. The coquette knows this consciously; every innocent girl knows this unconsciously, just as animals know it.

"Hence these abominable jerseys, these bustles, these naked shoulders, arms, and almost bosoms. Women, especially those that have been through the school of marriage, know very well that talk on the highest topics is just talk; that what man wants is the body and everything which displays it in a deceptively captivating light. And they act accordingly. If we should once forget this indecency which has become second nature and look at the life of our upper classes as it really is, in all its shamelessness, it would appear like one luxurious brothel. Don't you agree with me? I will prove it to you," he continued, not allowing me a chance to speak.

"You say that the women in our society live for other purposes than the women in the brothels. I say that is not so and I will prove it to you. If people differ in their purposes, in the internal contents of their lives, then this difference will also be shown externally, and externally people will be different. But look at these unhappy, despised women, and then look at the ladies of our highest social circles—the same decorations, the same fashions, the same perfumes, the same bare shoulders, arms, and bosoms, the same excessive exhibition of the bustle, the same passion for precious stones, for costly brilliant things, the same gaieties, dances and music and singing. The methods of allurement used by the ones are used by the others.

CHAPTER VII

"Yes, I was captured by these jerseys and curls of hair and bustles.

"And it was very easy to capture me, because I had been brought up under those conditions in which young people are quickly matured, like cucumbers grown in a hotbed. You see, our too abundant and energizing food, coupled with a completely idle existence, is nothing but a systematic incitement to lust. You may be surprised or not, but it is so. I myself have seen nothing of this sort until recently, but now I have seen it. This is the very thing that troubles me, that no one recognizes this and that everyone says stupid things like that woman who just got out.

"Yes, not far from where I live some peasants were working this spring on the railroad. The ordinary meals of the peasants are meager—bread, beer, onions; he is healthy and vigorous. When he goes to work on the railroad, his rations consist of buckwheat and one pound of meat. But he works it off with sixteen hours of hauling a thousand pounds on a wheelbarrow. And it is always so with him.

"But we who daily eat two pounds of meat and game and fish and all kinds of energy-giving foods and drinks—where does that go? In sensual excesses. If it goes that way, the safety valve is open and all is satisfactory; but close the safety valve—as I did temporarily—and immediately there will be an excitement which, coming through the prism of our artificial life, is expressed in a love that is full of idealism, sometimes even platonic. And so I fell in love as all young men do.

"Everything followed its course: raptures, emotions, poetry. In reality, this love of mine was the result, on the one hand, of the activity of her mother and the dressmakers; on the other, of the superabundance of stimulating food eaten by me in idleness. Had there not been excursions in boats, had there not been dressmakers to provide close-fitting gowns and the like, had my wife stayed home in a tasteless and formless gown; and had I, on the other hand, been a man in normal conditions, eating only as much food as I needed for my work, and had my safety valve been open—but then it happened to be temporarily closed—I would not have fallen in love and there would not have been any trouble.

CHAPTER VIII

"Well, so my rank, my fortune, my good clothes, the excursions in boats did the job. Twenty times it did not succeed, but this time it succeeded like a trap. I am not jesting. You see, nowadays marriages are always arranged—like traps. Do you see how natural it is? The girl has arrived at maturity and must be married. What could be simpler when the girl is not a monster and there are men who wish to get married? That is the way it used to be done. The girl reaches the right age; her parents arrange a marriage. So it has been done, throughout the world, among the Chinese, the Hindus, the Mohammedans, among the common Russian people—among at least ninety-nine per cent of the human race. It is only among a small one per cent, among us libertines and debauchees, that this custom has been found to be bad, and so we have invented another. Now, what is this new way? It is this: the girls sit round and the men come, as at a bazaar, to take their choice. And the girls wait and wonder and have their own ideas, but they dare not say, 'Dear sir, take me!' or, 'No, me!' or, 'Not her, but me!' or, 'Look at my shoulders and all the rest!'

"And we, the men, walk around and look them over and are quite smug. 'I know a thing or two, I won't be caught.' They go around, they look, they are satisfied that this is all arranged for their special pleasure. 'Look, but don't get taken in!' "

"What is to be done then?" I asked. "You would not expect the young women to make the offers, would you?"

"Well, I can't say exactly how; but if there is to be equality, then let it be equality. If the system of the matchmaker is considered humiliating, this is a thousand times more so! In the first case the rights and chances were equal, but in our method the woman is either a slave in a bazaar or the bait in the trap. Tell any mother or the girl herself the truth, that she is only occupied in husband-catching—my God, what an insult! But that is the truth and they have nothing else to do. And what is really dreadful is to see poor innocent young girls involved in all this. It wouldn't be so bad if it were done openly, but it is all deception. 'Ah, the origin of species, how interesting!' 'Lily is greatly interested in painting.' 'And will you be at the exhibition? How instructive!' And the carriage rides and the theater and the symphony. 'Oh, how remarkable!' 'My Lily is crazy about music!' 'And why don't you share these views?' And the boat rides. And always one thought: 'Take me!' 'Take my Lily!' 'No, me!' 'Just try your luck!' Oh, what vileness and falsehood!" he exclaimed, and, swallowing the last of his tea, proceeded to put away his utensils.

CHAPTER IX

"Do you realize," he began, while he was packing his tea and sugar in his bag, "the dominant power of women—the cause of the sufferings of the world—all proceeds from this?"

"How can you say 'the dominant power of women'?" I asked. "The rights, the majority of rights, belong to men."

"Yes, yes, that's the very point!" he exclaimed, interrupting me. "That's the very thing I wanted to say to you! And that is just what explains the extraordinary phenomenon that, on the one hand, woman is reduced to the lowest degree of humiliation while, on the other, she is the queen. Exactly as the Jews, by their power, avenge themselves for their humiliation, so it is with women. 'Ah, you want us to be merely merchants; very well, as merchants we will get you under our feet,' say the Jews. 'Ah, you wish us to be merely the objects of sensuality; very well, as objects of sensual pleasure we will make you our slaves,' say the women. A woman's lack of rights does not consist in the fact that she cannot vote or sit as judge—for rights are not embraced in any such activities—but in the fact that in sexual intercourse she is not the equal of a man: she does not have the right to enjoy a man or keep him at a distance according to her fancy; she cannot choose her husband according to her own desire instead of being the one chosen.

"You say that this would be unbecoming. Very good, then don't let the man have these rights. Now the woman lacks the right which the man has. And now, in order to get this right, she plays on the passions of man; by means of his passions, she subdues him so that, while seemingly he chooses, she is really the one. And having once learned this power, she abuses it and acquires a terrible control over men."

"Yes, but where is this special power?" I asked.

"Where? Everywhere! In everything! In any large city go into the shops—millions' worth there! Imagine the amount of human labor used in making those goods! But in ninety per cent of these shops what will you find for men? All the luxury of life is demanded and maintained by women. Count the factories! A vast proportion of them are manufacturing useless adornments—such as carriages, furniture, trinkets—for women. Millions of men, generations of slaves, perish in slave work in factories merely to satisfy the caprice of women. Women, like queens, hold ninety per cent of the human race as prisoners in slavery and hard labor. And all this because they have been kept down, deprived of their equal rights with men! And so they avenge themselves by taking advantage of our passions, by ensnaring us in their nets. Yes, everything comes from that.

"Women have made themselves such a weapon for attacking the senses of men that a man cannot be in a woman's company with any calmness. As soon as a man approaches a woman, he falls under the influence of her spell and grows foolish. I always used to feel painfully awkward when I saw a lady dressed up in a gown, but now it is absolutely terrifying! It is something dangerous for men and contrary to law. I feel almost a compulsion to call the police, to summon protection from the peril, to demand that the dangerous object be removed and put out of sight.

"You are laughing," he continued, "but this is no joke at all. I am convinced that the time is coming, and perhaps very soon, when men will recognize this and will be amazed that a society could exist in which things so disrupting of social calm were tolerated—those sensually provocative adornments of the body which we permit to women. It is exactly as though all kinds of traps were placed along our promenades and roads—it is worse than that! Why should games of chance be forbidden, but women who dress to appeal to the passions are not forbidden? They are a thousand times more dangerous!

CHAPTER X

"Now, then, you understand, I was what is called 'in love.' I not only imagined her as absolute perfection, I also imagined myself at the time of my marriage as absolute perfection. You see, there is no scoundrel who cannot—if he searches hard enough—find a scoundrel in some respects worse than himself, and so he finds an excuse for pride and self-satisfaction. So it was with me: I was not marrying for money, it was not a question of advantage with me (as it was with most of my acquaintances, who married either for money or connections). I was rich; she was poor. That was one thing. Another thing which gave me reason for pride was the fact that, while other men married with the intention of continuing to live in the same polygamy as they had enjoyed up to the time of their marriage, I had firmly resolved to live after my marriage as a monogamist—and my pride had no bounds in consequence of this resolution. Yes, I was a swine, but I saw myself as an angel!

"The time between my engagement and my marriage was not very long. But I cannot remember that period without shame. How vile it was! Love, you see, is represented as spiritual and not sensual. Well, if it is spiritual, if it is a spiritual communion, then it ought to be expressed in words, in conversations. There was nothing of this. It was awfully hard to talk when we were alone together. What a labor of Sisyphus it used to be! No sooner had we thought of something to say and said it than we would have to be silent until we could think of something else. There just was nothing to talk about. Everything that might be said of the life ahead of us—our arrangements, our plans—had been said. What more was there? You see, if we had been animals, then we would have known that we were not expected to talk; but here, on the contrary, it was necessary to talk, but there was nothing to say because what really interested us could not be expressed in words.

"Moreover, there was that abominable custom of eating bonbons, that coarse gluttony, and all those vile preparations for marriage—discussions about the house, the rooms, the beds, about nightgowns, linen, and so on. Now you must admit that if marriages were arranged in accordance with the *Domostroy*, the bedding, the dowry, the bed, and all that sort of thing would be mere particulars connected with the sacrament. But among us, when nine out of ten men who go to the altar do not believe in the sacrament and do not even believe that what they are doing is binding; when out of a hundred men there is scarcely one who has not been married before, and out of fifty not more than one who is not ready to deceive his wife on any convenient pretext; when the majority regard going to church as merely a special condition for possession of a certain woman—think what a terrible significance, in view of all this, all these details must have! It comes to be something in the nature of a sale. They sell the innocent girl to the libertine and they surround the sale with certain formalities.

CHAPTER XI

"That is the way everyone gets married. That is the way I got married, and the much-vaunted honeymoon began. What a vile name that is in itself!" he hissed bitterly. "Once, when I was making a tour of the sights of Paris, I went in to see the bearded woman and a water dog. She turned out to be a man in a low-necked dress, and the other turned out to be a dog wrapped in a walrus skin swimming in a bathtub. The whole thing was very far from interesting, but as I left, the showman conducted me out very obsequiously, and, addressing the people around the entrance, he pointed to me and said, 'Here, ask this gentleman if it is not worth looking at! Come in, come in, one franc apiece!'

"I was ashamed to say that it was not worth looking at, and the showman evidently counted on that. So it is, undoubtedly, with those who have experienced all the vileness of the honeymoon and yet do not disillusion others. I also refrained from dispelling anyone's illusions. But now I don't see why one should not tell the truth. It even seems to me that it is important to tell the truth. It was awkward, shameful, vile, pitiable, and above all it was boring, unspeakably boring. It was something like what I experienced when learning to smoke, when I was sick at my stomach and salivated, but I swallowed it and pretended it was very pleasant. Just as from that, the delights of marriage, if there are any, will follow. The husband must educate his wife in this vice in order to derive any pleasure from it."

"Vice? What do you mean?" I asked. "Why, you are talking about one of the most natural human functions!"

"Natural?" he exclaimed. "Natural? No! I have come to the conviction that it is not natural. In fact, it is utterly unnatural. Ask children! Ask an innocent young girl!"

"Unnatural?"

"It is natural to eat. It is agreeable, easy, pleasant, not at all shameful to eat; but this is vile and shameful and painful. No, it is not natural. And the pure maiden, I am convinced, will always hate it."

"But how," I asked, "would the human race be perpetuated?"

"Well, why shouldn't the human race perish?" he asked, with a touch of savage bitterness, as if he were expecting my unfair reply and as if he had heard it before. "Preach abstinence from procreation so that English lords may gormandize, and that's fine! Preach abstinence from procreation for the sake of giving a greater pleasure, and that's fine! But try to persuade people to refrain from procreation in the name of morality—ye gods, what an outcry! The human race would not be extinguished by an attempt to keep men from being swine." Then, pointing to the lamp, he continued, "Excuse me but this light bothers me. May I shade it?"

I said that it didn't matter to me, and then—hastily, as in everything he did—he stepped up on the seat and pulled the woolen shade down over the lamp.

"Nevertheless," I said, "if all men took this view, the human race would be annihilated."

He did not reply immediately.

"You ask how the human race would be perpetuated," he said, again taking his seat opposite me, spreading his legs wide apart and resting his elbows on his knees. "Why should it be continued—this human race?"

"Why? Otherwise there would be no more of us."

"Well, why should there be?"

"What a question. Why, to live, of course!"

"But why should we live? If there is no other aim, if life was given only to perpetuate life, then there is no reason why we should live. And if this is so, then the Schopenhauers and Hartmanns, and the Buddhists[6] as well, are perfectly right. If there is a purpose in life, it is clear that life ought to end when that purpose is attained. This is the logic of it," he said with evident agitation and seeming to set a high value on this thought. "This is the logic of it. If the aim of mankind is happiness, goodness, love—if you prefer; if the aim of mankind is what is said in the prophecies, that all men are to unite in universal love, that the spears are to be beaten into pruning hooks and the like, then what stands in the way of the attainment of this aim? Human passions do! Of all passions, the most powerful and vicious and obstinate is sexual, carnal love; and so, if passions are annihilated and with them the most powerful—carnal love—then the prophecy will be fulfilled. Men will be united, the aim of mankind will have been attained, and there will no longer be any reason for existence. As long as humanity exists, this ideal will exist, and, of course, this is not the ideal of rabbits or pigs (which is to propagate as rapidly as possible), and it is not the ideal of monkeys or Parisians (which is to enjoy all the refinements of sexual passion), but it is the ideal of goodness attained by self-restraint and chastity. Toward this people are striving, and always have striven. And see what follows.

"It follows that sexual love is the safety valve. If the human race has not as yet attained this aim, it is simply because there are passions, the strongest being sexual. But since there is sexual passion, a new generation comes along; and so there is always the possibility that the aim may be attained by some succeeding generation. But there will be generations until the aim is attained, until the prophecies are fulfilled, until all men are joined in unity. And then what would be the result?

"If it be granted that God created men for the attainment of a certain end, then He must have created them mortal and without sexual passion, or immortal. If they were mortal but without sexual passion, then what would be the result? This: that they would live without attaining their aim, and then would die; to attain the aim, God would have to create new men. But if they were immortal, then let us suppose—although it is harder for the same men to correct mistakes and approach perfection than it is for new generations—let us suppose, I say, that they reached their goal after many thousand years. But why should they? What good would the rest of their lives be to them? It is better as it is!

"But perhaps you do not agree with this reasoning. Perhaps you are an evolutionist. Even then it comes to the same thing. The highest genus of animals, men, in order to survive the conflict with other creatures, must band together like bees and not propagate irregularly; man must also, like the bees, nourish the sexless ones; in other words, man must struggle toward continence and never allow the kindling of carnal lust, to which the whole arrangement of our life is now directed."

He paused.

"Will the human race come to an end? Can anyone who looks at the world as it is have the slightest doubt? Why, it is as certain as death! We find the end of the world foretold in all the teachings of the Church, and in all the teachings of science it is likewise shown to be inevitable.

CHAPTER XII

"In our society it is exactly reversed: If a man has felt it incumbent on him to be continent during his bachelorhood, then after he is married he always feels it no longer necessary to restrain himself. You see, the honeymoons—this retirement to solitude which young people with the blessings of their parents practice—are nothing but a sanction for lewdness. But the moral law when broken brings its own punishment.

"In spite of all my efforts to make my honeymoon a success, it was a failure. The whole time was merely vile, shameful, and tiresome. And very soon it also became painfully oppressive. This state of things began very early. It was on the third or fourth day, I think, I found my wife depressed. I began to ask what was the matter and began to put my arms around her, which I supposed was all she could possibly desire. But she pushed away my arm and burst into tears.

"What was wrong? She could not say exactly, but she was depressed and downhearted. Probably her highly wrought nerves whispered to her the truth about the baseness of our relations, but she could not put it into words. I began to question her. She said something about being homesick for her mother. It seemed to me that this was not the truth. I tried to console her, but said nothing about her mother. I didn't realize that she was simply depressed and that her mother was merely a pretext.

"But she immediately complained because I said nothing about her mother, as if I didn't believe her. She told me she could see I didn't love her. I accused her of caprice and immediately her face changed; in place of melancholy appeared exasperation, and she began in the bitterest terms to accuse me of egotism and cruelty.

"I looked at her. Her whole face expressed the utmost coldness and hostility, almost hatred. I remember how alarmed I was on seeing this. 'How is this? What does it mean?' I asked myself. 'Love is the union of souls, and what have we here? Why, it cannot be! This is not she!'

"I did my best to soothe her, but I came up against such an insuperable wall of cold, venomous hostility that, before I had time to think, something like exasperation took hold of me too, and we said many disagreeable words to each other. The impression of this first quarrel was horrible. I called it a quarrel, but it was not really a quarrel; it was only the discovery of the gulf which was in reality between us. Our passionate love had worn itself out in the satisfaction of the senses, and we now remained facing each other as we really were—two egotists, alien to each other and desirous of getting the greatest possible pleasure out of the other!

"I called what took place between us a quarrel, but it was not a quarrel; it was only the consequence of the cessation of our sensuality, disclosing our real relation to each other. I did not realize that this cold and hostile relationship was our true one. I did not realize it then because our hostility, in the first weeks of our marriage, was soon hidden again from us by a new wave of sensuality, of passionate love.

"I thought that we had quarreled and made up, and that this would be the end of it. But in the very first month, during our honeymoon, there came another period of satiety; again we stopped being necessary to each other and another quarrel ensued. The second quarrel surprised me even more than the first. I said to myself, 'The first, then, was no mere exception; it will happen again and again.'

"The second quarrel surprised me especially because it had the most ridiculous cause—a minor matter involving money. I had never grudged money—and certainly never to my wife. I only remember that she made some remark of mine seem to show my desire to control her through money to which I claimed an exclusive right—something impossible, stupid, cowardly, and natural neither to her nor to me.

"I grew angry and reproached her for her insulting opinion of me. She returned the charge, and so it continued. And I observed in her words and in the expression of her face and eyes the same harsh, cold hostility that had surprised me the first time. I remember quarrels with my brother, my friends, even my father, but never did there arise such a venomous anger as now. But after a short time our hatred was concealed again by our passionate love, our sensuality, and once more I cherished the notion that these quarrels had simply been mistakes.

"But when the third and the fourth quarrel followed, I came to believe that they were not mere exceptions but that they would continue to occur. I was horror-struck at the future before me. I was tormented, too, by the horrible idea that I was the only person who had this misfortune, that other couples had no such experiences as I was having with my wife. I had not then found out that this is a common lot—that all men think, just as I did, that it is their exclusive misfortune and so conceal this shameful misfortune not only from others but also from themselves, being unwilling to acknowledge it.

"It began with us at the very first, it kept on all the time, and it grew more severe and more bitter. In the depths of my soul I felt from the very first that I was lost, that marriage had not turned out at all as I had expected, that it was not only not happiness but something very oppressive. But like all other men, I was not willing to acknowledge this—and I wouldn't acknowledge it even now were it not for the sequel. I concealed it not only from others but even from myself.

"Now I am amazed that I did not recognize my real position. It might have been seen in the fact that our quarrels arose from causes so minor that afterward, when they were ended, it was impossible to remember what brought them about. Our reason was not quick enough to offer sufficient pretexts for the hostility that constantly existed between us.

"But still more amazing was the insufficiency of the pretexts for reconciliation. Occasionally it was a word or an explanation, even tears, but sometimes—oh, how disgusting when I remember it now!—after the bitterest words were exchanged, suddenly there would come silence, glances, smiles, kisses, embraces! Fu! How awful! Why did I fail to see the vileness of all this even then . . . ?"

CHAPTER XIII

Two new passengers entered and settled themselves at the far end of the carriage. He stopped speaking while they were taking their places, but as soon as they became quiet he went on with his story, never for an instant losing the thread of his thoughts.

"What is vilest about this," he went on, "is that in theory love is something ideal and elevated, whereas in practice love is something low and swinish—something shameful and disgusting to mention or remember. You see, it was not without reason that nature made it shameful and disgusting . . . and, as such, it should be recognized and known by all. But we, on the contrary, pretend that what is low and shameful and disgusting is beautiful and elevated.

"What were the first symptoms of my love? They were that I gave myself up to animal excesses, not only feeling no shame but feeling a certain pride about them, not thinking either of her spiritual life or even of her physical life. I wondered what caused our animosity toward each other, when the thing was perfectly clear: this animosity was nothing else than the protest of human nature against the animal which was crushing it! I was amazed at our hatred of each other. But it could not have been otherwise. This hatred was identical with the mutual hatred felt by accomplices in a crime, both for the instigation and for the accomplishment of the deed. What else was it than a crime, when she, poor thing, became pregnant in the first month and our swinish relations continued?

"You think I am wandering from my story? Not at all. I am telling you how I killed my wife. At my trial I was asked *why* and *how* I killed her. Fools! They thought I killed her with a dagger on the seventeenth of October. I did not kill her then; it was long before. In exactly the same way that men are all killing their wives right now, all, all . . ."

"What do you mean?" I asked.

"It is amazing that no one is willing to know what is so clear and evident—what doctors ought to know and to proclaim, but they hold their tongues. It is simply this: men and women are like animals, and they are so created that after sexual union there is pregnancy and later suckling—both being conditions during which sexual union is dangerous for the woman and the child. The number of women and of men is about even: what does that mean? Of course it is clear: it doesn't take great wisdom to draw the same conclusion which animals draw—that continence is necessary. But no! Science has advanced so far as even to discover certain corpuscles which run about in the blood and all sorts of other useless stupidities, but it cannot comprehend this yet. At least there is no indication that science is recognizing this.

"And there are only two methods of escape for women: one is by making monsters of themselves, by destroying in themselves, according to the requirements of the case, the capacity of being women—that is, mothers—so that men may have no interruption of their enjoyment. The second escape is not an escape at all, but a simple, brutal, direct violation of the laws of nature. This is constantly taking place in all so-called good families, and it is that the woman, in direct opposition to her nature, is obliged while bearing or nursing a child to be at the same time her husband's mistress, is obliged to be what no other animal ever permits. And she can't have the strength for it!

"Hence in our social sphere you find hysteria and nerves, and among the masses you find 'possessed' women. You have observed among girls, pure girls I mean, there is no such thing as 'possession'; it is only among peasant women who live with their husbands. So it is here, and it is exactly the same all over Europe. The hospitals are full of hysterical women who have broken the laws of nature. These 'possessed' women and the patients of Charcot⁷ are complete cripples, but the world is full of half-crippled women. Think, what a mighty thing is taking place in a woman when she has conceived or when she is nursing a baby! That which is growing is to continue ourselves, is to take our place. And this holy function is violated—for what? It is terrible to think about it. And yet they talk about the freedom and the rights of women! It is as if cannibals should enjoy their prisoners as food while asserting that they were working for their freedom and rights."

All this was novel and surprising to me.

"But what *would* you do?" I asked. "If it were otherwise, a husband could have intercourse with his wife only once in two years. But a man . . ."

"Yes, yes, a man must have it," he broke in, taking the words out of my mouth. "Again, the priests of science support you in your views. Tell a man that vodka, tobacco, opium are indispensable to him, and it will indeed become indispensable to him! It seems that God did not understand what was needful and that therefore, since He did not ask advice of the magi, He arranged things badly. The thing does not hang together! It is indispensable for a man to satisfy his carnal desires—so they decide—but the whole business of conception and nursing babies hinders the satisfaction of this necessity. How is the difficulty to be overcome? How can we manage it? Go to the magi, of course! They will arrange it! They have thought it all through! Oh, when will these magi be dethroned, along with their deceptions! It is time! You see how far things have already gone: people go mad and shoot themselves, and all from this one cause. And how could it be otherwise? Animals seem to know that their progeny perpetuate their kind, and they observe a certain law in this respect. Only man lacks the wisdom to know this, and does not want to know it! All he cares for is to have the greatest possible pleasure. And who is he? He is the ruler of nature! He is man!

"Notice this: that animals enjoy intercourse only when there is to be progeny, but the vile ruler of nature does it only for pleasure's sake, and at any time. Moreover, he idealizes this monkeylike business, and calls it the pearl of creation, love! And in the name of this love, this vileness, he destroys—what? Half of the human race! In the name of his gratifications he makes of all women, who ought to be his partners in the progress of humanity toward truth and happiness, enemies instead! Look around and tell me who everywhere acts as a hindrance to the progress of humanity—women! And what makes them so? Nothing but this! Yes, yes," he repeated several times. He shifted his position, got out his cigarettes and began to smoke, evidently trying to calm himself a little.

CHAPTER XIV

"Thus I lived like a pig," he continued, in his former tone. "The worst of it was that while I was living this vile life, I imagined that, because I did not commit adultery with other women, I was leading a perfectly virtuous family life, that I was a moral and blameless man, that if we had our quarrels she was to blame—it was her character!

"She was not to blame, of course. She was like all other women. She had been brought up in the way required by the role of women in our society, and therefore educated as all women of the leisure class are.

"They talk nowadays about some newfangled method of female education. All idle words: the training of women is exactly what it must be in view of the notion of women universally held. The education of women will always correspond to the notion of her held by men. Now we all know what that is, how men look on women: Wine, Women, and Song, and all the rest of that stuff in the verses of the poets. Take all poetry, all painting, all sculpture, beginning with erotic verse and naked Venuses and Phrynes,[8] and you will see that woman is an instrument of pleasure. She is that on Truba and Grachevka[9] and she is that at a royal ball. And mark the devil's subtlety: pleasure, satisfaction . . . then let it be understood that it is merely pleasure, that woman is a sweet morsel. In the early days, knights boasted that they made goddesses of women, worshiped them at the same time that they looked on them as instruments of pleasure. But nowadays men declare that they respect women—some relinquish their seats to them or pick up their handkerchiefs, others admit women's right to hold responsible positions, to take part in government and the like. They do all this, but their view of them is always the same: woman is still the instrument of enjoyment and her body is the means of enjoyment. And she knows all that! It is just the same as slavery.

"Slavery is nothing else than the enjoyment by the few of the compulsory labor of the many. In order for slavery to come to an end, people must stop wanting to take advantage of the compulsory labor of others. They must consider it sinful or shameful. But while they abolish the external form of slavery, while they make it no longer possible to buy and sell slaves in the market—and they persuade themselves fully that slavery is abolished—they do not see and they do not wish to see that slavery still exists, because people, just the same as ever, like to profit by the labors of others, and they consider it fair and honorable to do so. As long as they consider this fair, there will always be men stronger and keener than others who will be able to do so.

"So it is with the emancipation of women. The slavery of woman consists in precisely this, that men choose to take advantage of her as an instrument of enjoyment and consider it right to do so.

"Well, and now they emancipate woman, they give her all the same rights as men, but they still regard her as an instrument of enjoyment, so they educate her, both in childhood and later by public opinion, with this end in view. But she remains the same depraved slave as before and her husband the same depraved slave-owner.

"They emancipate woman in the colleges and in the law courts, but they still look on her as an object of enjoyment! Train her, as she is trained among us, to regard herself in this light, and she will always remain a lower creature. Either she will, with the assistance of conspiring doctors, prevent the birth of her offspring—in other words, she will be a kind of prostitute, degrading herself not to the level of a beast but to the level of a thing—or she will be what she is in the majority of cases, heartsick, hysterical, unhappy, without hope of spiritual life.

"Schools and universities cannot change this. It can be changed only by a change in the way men regard women, and in the way women regard themselves. It can be changed only when woman considers virginity as the noblest condition and not, as it is now, a mark of failure and a disgrace. Until this comes about, the ideal of every girl, whatever her education, will remain that of attracting as many men as possible, as many males as she can, so that she can have a choice.

"The fact that this girl understands mathematics and that one plays on the harp does not change matters in the least. A woman is content and satisfied when she obtains a husband, so the chief task of woman is to learn how to snare and bewitch him. So it has been, and so it will be. Just as this is characteristic of the maiden's life in our circle, so it continues to be even after she is married. In the maiden's life this is necessary in order to get a choice; in the married woman's life it is necessary in order to get power over her husband.

"The only thing which changes this—or curtails it for the time being—is the birth of children. This is when she is not a monster, when she nurses her children. But here again the doctors interfere. In the case of my wife, although she wanted to suckle her first baby—she did suckle the next four—the state of her health seemed precarious, so the doctors, who cynically undressed her and felt her all over—for which service I was obliged to be grateful to them and to pay money— these gentle doctors decided she should not nurse her child. So, on her first opportunity, she was deprived of the sole means of saving herself from coquetry. She hired a wet nurse; in other words, we took advantage of the poverty, need, ignorance of another woman, lured her away from her own child to ours, and gave her in payment a headdress with lace. But that is not the point. The point is that during this period of emancipation from bearing and nursing babies, the female coquetry, which had hitherto lain dormant, manifested itself in her with greater strength. Correspondingly there appeared in me with special power the pangs of jealousy, which tore me unceasingly all my married life, as they cannot fail to tear all husbands who live with their wives as I lived with mine—unnaturally.

CHAPTER XV

"During the whole of my married life I never stopped suffering the pangs of jealousy, but there were times when I suffered from them with special acuteness. One such period was after the birth of my first child, when the doctors forbade my wife to nurse it. I was especially jealous at this time; in the first place, because my wife suffered from that uneasiness characteristic of mothers when there is an interruption of the regular course of life; secondly, because when I saw how easily she renounced the moral responsibilities of a mother I naturally, even though unconsciously, concluded that it would be equally easy for her to renounce the duties of a wife, especially since she was perfectly healthy, and, notwithstanding the dear doctors, nursed the other children, nursed them excellently."

"You obviously don't like doctors?" I said, having noticed the particularly bitter tone in his voice every time he mentioned them.

"This is not a matter of love or hate. They ruined my life, as they have ruined and will continue to ruin the lives of thousands, hundreds of thousands, of people. I cannot help connecting cause and effect. I am aware that they, like lawyers and others, must earn money to live on. I would willingly give them half my income—and, if it were realized what the doctors are doing, everyone else would also, I am convinced, give half his property on condition that they would not meddle with our family lives, that they would never come near us. I have never collected any statistics, but I know of dozens of cases—a multitude of them—in which they have killed the unborn child, declaring that the mother would not live if the child were born, and yet afterward the mother was perfectly fortunate in childbearing; or again, they have killed the mother under the pretext of some operation or other. No one reckons up these murders, just as no one ever reckoned the murders of the Inquisition, because it has been supposed that this was done for the benefit of humanity. It is impossible to count the crimes committed by them. But all these crimes are nothing compared to the moral corruption of materialism which they introduce into the world, especially through women.

"I say nothing about the fact that, if we should follow their prescription, then, thanks to the infection everywhere and in everything, people would have to separate rather than draw closer together. They would, according to the teachings of the doctors, have to sit apart and never let the atomizer with disinfectant out of their mouths. Lately, however, they have discovered that even this is of no special help!

"But this is not the point. The principal poison lies in the demoralization of the people, of women especially. Today, it is no longer enough to say, 'You are living a bad life; live better.' You can't say that to yourself or to another. If you are living a bad life, the cause lies in the abnormal state of the nerves, and the like! And so you have to consult the doctors, and they prescribe an expensive medicine from the drugstore, and you take it! You grow worse . . . so you take new drugs and consult other doctors. An excellent racket!

"But that is not what I'm getting at. I only say that she nursed the other children admirably, that the only thing that saved me from the pangs of jealousy was her bearing and nursing the children. If it had not been for that, the inevitable end would have come about earlier. The children saved me and her. In eight years she gave birth to five children, and she nursed all except the first herself."

"Where are your children now?" I asked.

"My children?" he repeated, with a startled look.

"Forgive me! Perhaps I caused you painful memories."

"No, it's no matter. My sister-in-law and her brother took charge of my children. They have refused to return them to me. You see, I am a kind of insane man. I have just seen them, but they won't give them to me because, if they did, I would educate them so that they would not be like their parents. But they feel it is necessary that the children should be the same as their parents. Well, what can one do? I can understand why they don't give them to me or trust me. Besides, I don't know that I'd have the strength to bring them up. I think not. I am a wreck, a cripple! One thing I have: I know. Yes, it is clear that I know what the rest of the world does not yet know.

"Yes, my children are growing up to be just such savages as all the others around them are. I have seen them—three times I have seen them. I can't do anything for them—not a thing. I am now going to my place in the south; there I have a cottage and a little garden.

"Yes, it will be long before people know what I now know. It will soon be easy to find out how much iron and what other metals there are in the sun and the stars, but what will cure our swinishness? That is hard, very hard!

"You, at least, have listened to me, and for that I am grateful.

CHAPTER XVI

"You mentioned the children. There, again, what terrible lying goes on about children! 'Children are a divine benediction.' 'Children are a delight.' That is all a lie. They used to be so but now there is nothing of the sort, nothing at all. Children are a torment, nothing less! The majority of mothers feel so, and some of them do not hesitate to say so. Ask the greater number of the mothers of our circle—people of means—and they will tell you that they do not wish to have children because the children may get sick and die. If they are born, they do not want to suckle them because they may grow too devoted to the children and suffer sorrow. The delight which the child affords them by its beauty, its tiny little arms, its little feet, its whole body—the satisfaction is less than the agony, not from illness or loss of the child, but from the mere worry about the possibility of illness and death. Having weighed the advantages and disadvantages, it seems disadvantageous, and therefore not desirable, to have children. They say this openly, boldly, imagining that these sentiments grow out of their love for their children—good, praiseworthy feelings in which they take pride. They do not notice this: that by such reasoning they directly renounce love and assert their selfishness. For them there is less pleasure from the charm of a child than suffering from worry about it; therefore they don't want a child which they would come to love. They do not sacrifice themselves for the beloved creature, but they sacrifice the beloved creature for themselves.

"It is clear that this is not love, but selfishness. But it is not for me to criticize these mothers of well-to-do families for their selfishness when I think of all they endure for the sake of the health of their children in our modern fashionable life, thanks again to the doctors. How well I remember even now our life during the first period of our marriage, when we had three or four young children and when my wife was absorbed with them! It fills me even now with horror!

"It was no kind of a life. It was a perpetual hazard, rescue from one peril followed by new peril; then new and desperate endeavors, then a new rescue—all the time as if we were on a sinking ship! It sometimes seemed to me that this was done on purpose, that she was pretending to be troubled about her children so as to get the upper hand of me, so simply and pleasingly were questions decided to her advantage. It seemed to me sometimes that all she said and did in these circumstances was pretended. But no! She herself suffered terribly and kept tormenting herself about the children, about their health and their illnesses. It was a torture for her and for me also. It was impossible for her not to torment herself.

"You see, her attachment to her children—the animal instinct to nurse them, to fondle them, to protect them—was in her as it is in the majority of women; but she had not what animals have—freedom from imagination and reason. The hen has no fear of what may befall her chick; she knows nothing about the diseases which may afflict it, knows nothing of all those remedies which men imagine they can employ to keep away sickness and death. And so the young ones are no torment to the hen. She does for chicks what is natural and pleasant for her to do; her young are a delight to her. When her chick shows signs of sickness, her duties are distinctly determined: she warms and nourishes it. And in doing this she knows that she is doing her duty. If the chick dies, she does not ask herself why it died or where it has gone to. She cackles for a while, and then goes on living as before.

"But for our unhappy women—and for my wife—there was nothing of the kind. Then, apart from the question of diseases and how to cure them, she had heard from all sides and had read endlessly varied and contradictory rules on how to educate them, how to develop them: you must feed it this way; no, not this way, but so; how to dress it, what to give it to drink, when to bathe it, when to put it to sleep, when to take it out to walk, how much fresh air—in regard to all this, we (and she especially) learned new rules every week. Just as if children began to be born only yesterday! If a child was not fed quite properly or wasn't bathed at the right time and it fell ill, it showed that we were to blame, that we had not done what we should have done. Even when children are well, they are a torment. But when they fall ill, it is perfect hell! It is supposed that sickness may be cured and that there is a science of healing and there are men—doctors—who know how to heal. Not that all know, but that the best of them do. And here is a sick child and it is necessary to get hold of this man, the very best of his profession, who can cure; the child is saved. But if you don't get hold of this doctor, or if you don't live where this doctor lives, then the child is lost. And this belief was not exclusively confined to my wife; it is the belief of all the women of her sphere, and on all sides she hears such talk as this: 'Two of Ekaterina Semenovna's children died because they did not call Ivan Zakharych in time, but Ivan Zakharych saved the life of Marya Ivanovna's oldest daughter; and the Petrov children were sent in time to different hotels by this doctor's advice, so their lives were saved; but those that had not been isolated, died. And such and such a woman had a feeble child, and by the doctor's advice they took it south, and it lived . . .'

"How can she fail to torment herself and be agitated all life long, when the life of her children, to whom she is devotedly attached, depends on her knowing in time what Ivan Zakharych will say about it? But no one knows what Ivan Zakharych will say—least of all, himself, because he knows very well that he knows nothing at all and cannot give any help and that he pontificates so that people will not stop believing in his knowledge.

"You see, if she had been simply an animal, she would not have tormented herself so. If she had been a normal human being, she would have had faith in God, she would have thought and spoken as true believers say: 'The Lord gave, and the Lord hath taken away—and one can't escape from God.'

"So our whole life with our children was no joy but a torment for her, and therefore for me also. How could we help tormenting ourselves? And she did constantly torture herself. It used to be that just as we were calming down from a scene of jealousy or a simple quarrel and were planning to start to read something or do something, word would suddenly be brought that Vasya was vomiting, that Masha had diarrhea, or that Andrusha had a rash—and the end of it was that we had no kind of life. Where should we send? What doctor should we get? In which room should we isolate the patient? And then began enemas, temperatures, medicines, doctors. And this would scarcely be done before something else would begin. There was no regular family life. But as I have told you, there was a constant apprehension from real or fancied dangers. And that is the way it is in most families. In my family it was especially pronounced. My wife was dedicated to the children and believed every bit of advice and warning.

"Thus it was that the presence of children not only failed to improve our life but poisoned it. Moreover, the children gave us new pretexts for quarreling. From the time we began to have children—and even more frequently as they grew—our children became the very means and object of our quarrels. They were not only the subject but the very instrument of dissension. We fought each other with our own children as weapons. Each of us had his own favorite child as an instrument of attack. I made more use of Vasya, the eldest, she of Lisa. Later, when the children began to grow up, they took sides according to which one of us was able to attract them. They suffered terribly from the state of affairs, poor little things, but we had no time to think of them in our incessant warfare. The little girl was my special ally; the oldest boy, who resembled his mother and was her favorite, often seemed hateful to me.

CHAPTER XVII

"Well, thus we lived. Our relations grew more and more hostile, and at last it went so far that difference of views no longer produced enmity, but enmity itself produced difference of views. Whatever she said, I was ready in advance to disagree with her, and so it was with her.

"In the fourth year it was admitted by both of us, though tacitly, that we could not understand each other—that we could not agree. We stopped trying to talk anything over to the end. In regard to the simplest things, especially the children, we each kept our own opinion unchangeably. As I now remember, the opinions I held were not so precious that I could not have given them up; but she had opposing notions, and to yield to them meant to yield to her. And this I could not do. Nor could she yield to me. She evidently considered herself always perfectly right toward me, and, as for me compared to her, I was always a saint in my own eyes. When we were together we were practically reduced to silence or to such conversations as animals probably carry on together: 'What time is it?' 'Is it bedtime?' 'What will you have for dinner today?' 'Where will you drive?' 'What is the news?' 'We must send for the doctor; Masha has a sore throat.'

"It required only a step of a hair's width beyond this unendurably narrowing circle of conventional sentences to inspire a quarrel—skirmishes and expressions of hatred about the coffee, the tablecloth, the drive, a play at whist—in fact, over trifles which could not have had the slightest importance for either of us. In me, at least, hatred of her boiled terribly. I often looked at her when she was drinking tea, dangling her crossed leg, bringing her spoon to her mouth to sip from it, swallowing—I hated her for this very trifle as if it were the worst of crimes. I did not notice that these periods broke out in me with regularity and uniformity, corresponding to the periods of what we called love. A period of love—then a period of hatred. An energetic period of passion—then a long period of hatred. A feebler show of passion—then a briefer outbreak of hatred.

"We did not then comprehend that this love and hatred were one and the same animal passion, only with opposite poles. It would have been horrible to live in this way if we had realized our situation; but we did not realize it and did not see it. In this lies the salvation, as well as the punishment, of a man—that, when he is living irregularly, he may blind himself so as not to see the wretchedness of his situation.

"Thus it was with us. She sought to forget herself in strenuous and absorbing occupations—her housekeeping, the arrangement of the furniture, dressing herself and the family, and the education and health of the children. I had my own affairs to attend to—drinking, hunting, playing cards, going to my office. We were both busy all the time. We both felt that the busier we were, the more justified we were in being annoyed with each other. 'It is very well for you to make up such grimaces,' I would think, mentally addressing her. 'You tormented me all night with your scenes, but now I have a meeting to attend.' 'It is all very well for you,' she would not only think, but even say aloud, 'but the baby kept me awake all night long.'

"These new theories of hypnotism, mental disease, and hysteria are all an absurdity—not a simple absurdity, a vile and pernicious one. Charcot would have infallibly said that my wife was a victim of hysteria and he would have said that I was abnormal, and he probably would have tried to cure us. But there was no disease to cure.

"Thus we lived in a continual mist, not recognizing the situation in which we found ourselves. And if the catastrophe which overtook us had not occurred, I should have continued to live on till old age in the same way, and on my deathbed I should even have thought that I had lived a good life—not remarkably good, but not at all a bad life—like that of all other men. I should never have understood that abyss of unhappiness and that abominable falsehood in which I was floundering.

"We were like two convicts fastened to one chain, hating each other, each poisoning the life of the other and striving not to recognize the fact. I did not then realize that ninety-nine per cent of the married people live in the same hell as mine, and that it must be so. Nor did I then realize that it was so of others or true of myself.

"It is amazing what coincidences may be found in a regular, and even in an irregular, life. Thus when parents are beginning to find that they are making each other's lives unendurable, it becomes imperative that they move to the city for the better education of their children. And so it was we found it necessary to move to the city."

He stopped speaking and twice he gave vent to those strange sounds which this time were more like repressed sobs. We were approaching a station.

"What time is it?" he asked.

I looked at my watch. It was two o'clock.

"Aren't you tired?" he asked.

"No, but you must be."

"I am suffocating. Excuse me, I will go out and get a drink of water."

He got up and went unsteadily through the carriage.

I sat alone, thinking over what he had told me, and became so absorbed in thought that I did not notice him when he returned through the door at the far end.

CHAPTER XVIII

"Yes, I keep wandering from my story," he began. "I have pondered over it a good deal. I look on many things in a different way from what most people do, and I want to talk it all out.

"Well, we began to live in the city. There a man may live a century and never realize that he has long ago died and rotted. One has no time to study himself—his time is wholly occupied: business, social relations, his health, art, the health of his children, their education. Now he must receive calls from such and such people; now he must return them; now he must see this woman; now he must hear that man. At any given moment there will surely be in the city one celebrity, generally several, whom it is impossible for you to miss. Now you have to consult a doctor for yourself or for this one or that; then you have to see one of the tutors or the governess, and so life is frittered away. Well, so it was we lived and seemed to suffer less from our life together. Moreover, we had at first the pleasant business of getting settled in a new city, in a new home, and then, later, in traveling back and forth between the city and the country.

"Thus we lived one winter. During the second winter the incident which I am going to relate took place. It seemed a trifling thing and we thought little about it then—still it led to all that followed.

"She became delicate in health, and the doctors forbade her to have any more children and they taught her how to prevent it. This was repulsive to me. I had no patience with such an idea, but with frivolous obstinacy she insisted on having her way and I had to yield. The last justification of the swinish life—children—was taken away. Our life became viler than ever.

"To the peasant, to the laboring man, children are a necessity; although it is hard for him to feed them, still he must have them and so the marital relations are justified. But to us, who already have children, more children are not desirable; they cause extra work, expense, further division of property—they are a burden. And therefore there is no justification for our swinish life. Either we artificially prevent the birth of children or we regard children as a misfortune—as the consequence of carelessness, which is worse.

"There is no justification. But we have fallen so low morally that we do not see the need for justification. The majority of men now belonging to the cultivated class give themselves up to this form of debauchery without the slightest twinge of conscience.

"No one feels any conscientious scruples, because conscience is a non-existent quality except—if we may so say—the 'conscience' of public opinion and of criminal law. And in this respect neither the one nor the other is violated; no one has to bear the brunt of public scorn, for all—including Marya Pavlovna and Ivan Zakharych—do the same thing. Why breed beggars or deprive oneself of the possibility of social life? Is there any reason to stand in awe of the criminal law or to fear it? Peasant girls and soldiers' wives throw their babies into ponds and wells and they must go to prison, but all that sort of thing is done by us properly and neatly!

"Thus we lived two years. The means used by the rascally doctors evidently began to take effect; physically she improved and grew more beautiful, like the last beauty of the summer. She was aware of this, and began to take special care of herself. Her beauty became fascinating and disturbing to men. She was in the prime of a woman of thirty and, since she was no longer bearing children, her figure filled out, stirring the passions. Even the sight of her was provocative. When she passed men she attracted all eyes. She was like a well-fed and bridled horse which had not been driven for some time and from which the bridle was taken off. There was no longer any restraint, as with ninety-nine per cent of our women. Even I felt this, and it was alarming."

CHAPTER XIX

He suddenly got up and sat down close by the window.

"Excuse me," he exclaimed, looking out intently for a few minutes. Then he sighed deeply and sat down opposite me again. His face had undergone a complete change: a sad look came into his eyes and a strange sort of smile curved his lips.

"I am a little tired, but I will go on with my story. There is plenty of time left; it has not begun to grow light yet. Yes," he began again, after he had lit a cigarette. "She grew fuller after she stopped bearing children, and her malady—the constant worriment over the children—began to disappear. It did not really disappear, but she awoke, as it were, from a drunken stupor; she began to remember and to see that there was a whole world, a divine world, with joys she had forgotten and in which she did not know how to live—a wonderful world which she did not understand at all! 'How to keep it from being wasted? Time is fleeting—it will not return.'

"Thus I imagined she thought, or rather felt, and indeed it would have been impossible for it to be otherwise. She had been educated to believe that in this world there is only one thing worthy of anyone's attention—love. She had become married, she had got some notion of what this love was, but it was far from what had been promised, from what she expected. She had undergone the loss of many illusions; she had borne many sufferings, and then that unexpected torment—so many children! This agony had worn her out. And now, thanks to the obliging doctors, she had discovered that it was possible to avoid having children. She was glad; she made the experiment and began to live for the one thing she knew—love. But the enjoyment of love with a husband consumed with fiery passions of wrath and jealousy was not the kind she wanted. She began to picture to herself another, a more genuine, a newer kind of connection—at least that is what I imagine was the case. And so she began to look around, expecting something.

"I noticed it and was deeply troubled. It kept happening all the time that she—talking as her habit was with me through the medium of others, talking with strangers but making her remarks for my ears— expressed herself boldly (never at all dreaming that she, an hour before, had said diametrically the opposite) and half seriously to the effect that maternal solicitude was a delusion, that there was no sense in sacrificing her life for her children, that she was still young and could still enjoy life. She now occupied herself less with the children, certainly with less untiring solicitude. She gave more and more attention to herself, to her external appearance (although she tried to keep it secret), to her pleasures, and to her accomplishments. She once more enthusiastically took up her piano, which she had entirely neglected. That was the beginning of the end."

Once more he turned his weary-looking eyes to the window, but soon, evidently making an effort to control himself, he proceeded.

"Yes, that man appeared."

He hesitated, and twice produced through his nose his peculiar sounds. I saw that it was difficult for him to mention that man, to recall him, even to allude to him. But he made an effort and, as though breaking through the barrier which hindered him, he resolutely went on.

"He was vile in my eyes, in my estimation. Not because he played an important part in my life, but because he was really vile. However, the fact that he was bad serves merely as proof of how irresponsible she was. If it had not been him, it would have been someone else."

He again stopped speaking.

"Yes, he was a musician, a violinist—not a professional musician, but a half-professional, half-society man. His father was a landowner, a neighbor of my father's. His father went to ruin, and his children— three of them were boys—all managed to make their way. Only this one, the youngest, was entrusted to his godmother in Paris. There he was sent to the Conservatoire because he had a talent for music, and he was graduated as a violinist and played in concerts. He was the man..."

It was evident that he was about to say something harsh but he restrained himself, and said, speaking rapidly: "Well, I don't know how he had lived up to that time, but that year he appeared in Russia and came to my house. He had glistening almond-shaped eyes, smiling lips, a little waxed mustache, the most fashionable method of styling his hair, an insipidly handsome face—such as women call 'not bad.' He had a slender build, not ill-shaped, and a large behind such as they say characterizes Hottentot women. This is musical! Slipping into familiarity as far as was permitted him, but sensitive and always ready to stop short at the slightest resistance, he was concerned mainly about external appearances, with that peculiar touch of Parisian elegance lent by buttoned boots and bright-colored neckties and everything else which foreigners acquire in Paris—and which always attract women. In his manners there was a posed external gaiety. He had a way, you know, of speaking about everything by hints and fragmentary allusions—as if the person with whom he was speaking knew all about it and could fill in the missing links.

"Well, then, this man with his music was the cause of all the trouble. You see, at the trial the whole affair was represented as having been caused by my jealousy. This was not so at all. That is, it was not exactly so. It was, and it was not. At the trial it was decided that I had been deceived and that I had committed the murder in defending my outraged honor—so they called it in their language—and on this ground I was acquitted. At the trial I did my best to explain my idea of it, but they assumed that I had wished to restore my wife's honor.

"Her relations with that musician, whatever they were, did not have that significance in my eyes nor in hers. It simply had the significance I have already mentioned: my swinishness. All came from the fact that between us existed that terrible gulf, of which I have told you, that terrible tension of mutual hatred whereby the first impulse was sufficient to precipitate a crisis. The quarrels between us, as time went on, became worse and were especially alarming because they were mingled with intense animal fury.

"If he had not appeared, someone else would. If there had not been one pretext for jealousy, there would have been another. I believe that all husbands living as I lived must either lead wanton lives, separate, or kill themselves—or their wives, as I did. If this does not occur, it is a rare exception. Before the end came, I was several times on the brink of suicide, and even she had tried to poison herself.

CHAPTER XX

"This is what happened not long before our crisis. We had been living in a sort of armistice, and there was no reason for it to be broken. Then one day we had a conversation during which I remarked that a certain dog had received a medal at an exhibition. She said, 'Not a medal, but honorable mention.' A dispute followed. We began to reproach each other, skipping from subject to subject. 'Well, I knew that long ago; it was always so.' 'You said so and so!' 'No, I said thus and so!' 'Do you mean to say I'm lying?'

"There is a feeling that you are on the edge of a frightful quarrel and that you will be tempted to kill yourself or her. You know that it will begin in an instant. You dread it like fire. You want to control yourself but anger seizes your whole being. She is in the same, even worse mood. She deliberately misinterprets every word you say; every word she speaks is steeped in venom. Wherever she knows I am most sensitive, there she strikes. The further the quarrel goes, the more vicious it gets. I shout, 'Shut up!' or something to that effect.

"She rushes from the room and takes refuge in the nursery. I try to hold her so that I may speak my piece and prove my position. I seize her by the arm. She pretends that I have hurt her, and screams, 'Children, your father is striking me!' I cry, 'You liar!' 'This is not the first time either,' she cries, or something to that effect.

"The children rush to her. She tries to calm them. I say, 'Don't put on an act!' She says, 'For you everything is pretense! You hit a woman and then say she is pretending. Now I understand you. This is the very thing you want!' I cry out, 'I wish you were dead!'

"I remember how horror-struck I was at those words. I would never have believed myself capable of uttering such coarse, terrible words; I am amazed that they leaped from my mouth. I blurt out those terrible words and rush into my study and sit down and smoke. I hear her in the vestibule, preparing to go out. I ask, 'Where are you going?' She does not reply.

" 'Then the devil with her!' I say to myself. I return to the study and again sit down and smoke. A thousand different plans—how to avenge myself on her, how to get rid of her, how to set everything to rights again, how to act as if nothing had taken place—go rushing through my brain.

"I sit and think, and I smoke steadily. I think of deserting her, of hiding myself, of going to America. I actually go so far as to dream of getting rid of her, and I think how delightful it would be as soon as this is accomplished to make new ties with a congenial woman, entirely new. I dream of getting rid of her by her death or by securing a divorce, and I figure how this may be brought about. I see that my mind is wandering, that I am not thinking logically, but to keep from seeing that I am thinking the wrong kind of thoughts, I smoke heavily.

"But life at home goes on. The governess comes and asks, 'Where is madame? When will she be back?' The butler asks, 'Shall I serve tea?'

"I go into the dining room. The children—especially the oldest one, Lisa, who is already old enough to understand—look at me questioningly, disapprovingly. We silently drink our tea. There is no sign of her. The evening passes; she does not come. Two thoughts mingle in my soul: wrath because she is tormenting me and the children by her absence—and yet, she will return in the end—and fear that she will not come back, that she will kill herself.

"I should go search for her. But where to find her? At her sister's? But it would be stupid to go there with such an inquiry. Well, then, let her go! If she wants to torment us, let her torment herself too. That is the very thing she would like me to do. And next time she will be even worse!

"But suppose she is not at her sister's, but has done something else—has even already killed herself?

"Eleven o'clock . . . twelve o'clock. I will not go to the bedroom—it would be stupid to lie down there and wait alone, but I will lie down where I am. I try to occupy myself with some work, to write letters, to read, but I can't do anything. I sit alone in my study, I torment myself with worries, I am full of anger. I listen. Three o'clock . . . four—no sign of her. I fall asleep just before dawn. When I wake up, there is still no sign of her.

"Everything in the house goes on as usual, but all are in a state of uncertainty and look questioningly and reproachfully at me, as though it is all my fault. And within me is still the same struggle—anger because she torments me and anxiety about her.

"About eleven o'clock in the morning her sister comes as her envoy. She begins in the usual way, 'She is in a terrible state of mind. Now what does it all mean? Something must have happened.'

"I speak about the incompatibility of her temper, and I assure her that I have done nothing. 'But you see that things cannot be allowed to go on this way,' she says. 'It is all her fault, not mine,' I reply. 'I will not take the first step. If it is to be a separation, then let it be a separation.'

"My sister-in-law goes away without getting any satisfaction. I spoke boldly that I would not take the first step, but as soon as she is gone, I see the poor, frightened children and I am already prepared to take the first step. I should even be glad to do so, but I don't know how. Again I pace up and down; I smoke; I fortify myself with vodka and wine. Finally I attain what I unconsciously sought: the inability to see the stupidity, the cowardice of my position.

"About three she returns. She sees me but says nothing. I imagine that she has come for a reconciliation, and I begin to tell her how I had been led on by her reproaches. She, with a harsh and harassed face, replies that she has not come to indulge in explanations but to take the children away—that we cannot possibly live together. I begin to explain that I was not the one to blame, that it was she who had driven me out of my senses. She looks at me sternly, triumphantly, and then says, 'Don't say any more; you have enough to be sorry for.' I reply that I cannot endure any comedy.

"Then she screams out something which I don't even understand clearly and runs to her room. She turns the key behind her; she has locked herself in. I knock . . . no answer. I wait, furious.

"Half an hour later Lisa comes running in with tears in her eyes. 'What has happened?' 'I can't hear Mama!'

"We go to her room. I push against the double door with all my might. The bolt happens to be only partly in, so both doors yield. I rush to the bed. She is lying on it in an awkward position in her petticoats and boots. On the table is an empty opium bottle. We bring her to consciousness. Tears and ultimate reconciliation. But it is no reconciliation. In each of us is the same old hatred—and now an additional sense of exasperation for the pain of this quarrel for which each blames the other. But this trouble must be somehow ended, and life goes on in its old ruts. But in the same way such quarrels, and even worse ones, take place regularly all the time—now every day—and it is always the same thing.

"One time I even applied for a foreign passport—the quarrel had lasted two days. But there was a semi-explanation, a semi-reconciliation, and I stayed.

CHAPTER XXI

"Such, then, were our relations when that man appeared. He came to Moscow—his name was Trukhashevsky—and he came to my house. It was in the morning. I received him. In former times we had been on familiar terms. He tried, sometimes using the more familiar form of address, to keep on his old footing of *thee* and *thou,* but I quickly settled the question by using the formal *you* and he immediately took the hint. Even at first glance he impressed me unfavorably. But some fatal power strangely impelled me not to keep him at a distance or to send him away, but rather to be more cordial to him. Why, what could have been simpler than to have talked coolly with him a few minutes and to have said good-bye without introducing him to my wife?

"But no. I talked with him about his playing and remarked that we had heard that he had given up the violin. He replied that on the contrary he was playing more now than ever before. He recalled the fact that I, too, had once played. I said that I had given up playing but that my wife played very well. Amazing! My feelings toward him that very first day—that very first hour of my meeting with him—were such as they could have been only after all that occurred subsequently. There was something strained in my relations with him; I noticed every word and every expression spoken by him or myself, and I attributed importance to them.

"I presented him to my wife. Immediately a conversation on music began between them and he offered to practice with her. My wife, as was the case with her in that period of her life, was very elegant and fascinating, captivatingly beautiful. He evidently impressed her at first sight. Moreover, she was delighted at the prospect of being accompanied by a violin, which she liked so much that she had once hired a violinist from the theater. Her face expressed this pleasure. But as soon as she saw me, she instantly understood how I felt about it; her expression changed and our game of mutual deceit began. I smiled pleasantly, pretending it was very agreeable to me. He, looking at my wife as all immoral men look at pretty women, pretended that he was interested in nothing else but the topic of conversation—especially that part which did not interest him at all. She tried to seem indifferent, but my falsely smiling expression of jealousy, so well known to her, and his lustful look evidently disturbed her. I saw that from his very first glance her eyes shone with peculiar brilliance, and, apparently as a consequence of my jealousy, there passed between them a kind of electric current that created a uniformity in the expression of their eyes and their smiles. She blushed; he blushed. She smiled; he smiled. They talked about music, about Paris, about all sorts of trifles. When he rose to leave, he stood smiling with his hat resting against his quivering thigh, and looked now at her, now at me, apparently waiting to see what we would do.

"I remember that moment especially because I might have refrained from inviting him to call again, and if I had, the trouble would not have happened. But I looked at him and her. 'Don't think for an instant that I am jealous of you,' I said mentally to her, 'or that I am afraid of you,' I said mentally to him. So I invited him to come some evening to play his violin with my wife. She looked at me in surprise, blushed, and, as if startled, began to plead that she did not play well enough. This refusal of hers irritated me still more, and I insisted on it with all the more vehemence. I remember the strange feeling I had as I looked at the back of his head and his white neck—contrasting strongly with his black hair which was combed back on both sides—as he left us with a springy gait, like that of a bird. I knew that this man's presence was a torture to me. 'It depends on me,' I said to myself, 'to act in such a way as never to see him again. But that would be a confession that I fear him. No, I do not fear him; it would be too humiliating.' And there in the vestibule, knowing that my wife was listening to me, I insisted that he come back that very evening and bring his violin with him. He promised he would and left.

"In the evening he came with his violin and they played together. For a long time the music did not go very well: we didn't have the pieces he wanted, and those he had my wife could not play without some practice. I was very fond of music and enjoyed their playing, arranging his music stand for him and turning his pages. They managed to play something—a few songs without words and a sonata by Mozart. He played excellently. He had magnificent tone—a delicate noble art entirely out of keeping with his character.

"He was, of course, far better than my wife, so he helped her and at the same time politely praised her playing. He behaved very well. My wife seemed interested only in the music, and was very simple and natural. Though I also pretended to be interested in the music, still I did not cease to be tortured by jealousy all the evening. From the first moment his eyes fell on my wife, I saw that the beast in them—beyond all the restrictions of their position and the society in which they lived—was asking, 'Is it possible?' and answering its own question with a 'Yes, certainly it is.' I saw that he had never expected to find my wife, a society lady of Moscow, such a fascinating creature, and that he was delighted. There was no doubt in his mind that she was willing. The main question was how the insufferable husband could be kept from interfering. If I myself had been pure I would not have understood this, but, like the majority of men, I had indulged in the same notions of women until I was married, so I could read his mind like a book.

"I was especially tormented by the fact that her feelings and mine were in a state of constant irritation interrupted only occasionally by our habitual sensuality; while this man, by his external elegance, by his novelty, by his great musical talent, by the rapport that came of their playing together, by the influence of music, especially a violin, on a very impressionable nature—all this, I say, made it inevitable that this man should please her . . . and more than that, that he should, without the least hesitation, conquer, overwhelm, fascinate, enchain, and do with her whatever he willed. I could not help seeing that, and I suffered painfully. But in spite of this, or possibly in consequence of it, some force compelled me against my will to be very polite and even cordial to him. Whether I did this to show my wife or to show him that I was not afraid, or whether I did it to deceive myself, I do not know—only I could not from the very first be natural with him. In order not to yield to my desire to kill him on the spot, I had to be friendly toward him. At dinner I treated him to expensive wines, I praised him for his playing, I talked with him with a particularly friendly smile, and I invited him to dinner the following Sunday, to play again with my wife. I said I would ask some of my musical friends to hear him. And so it went."

Pozdnyshev, under the powerful influence of his emotion, changed his position and emitted his peculiar sounds.

"It is strange what an effect the presence of that man had on me," he began once more, making an effort to regain his calm. "Two or three days later I came home from a business exhibition, and as I entered the vestibule I became conscious of a sudden feeling of oppression—as if a stone had been rolled on my heart—and I could not explain it to myself. It was due to the fact that, as I was passing through the vestibule, I noticed something which reminded me of him. Only when I reached my study did I realize what it was. I returned to the vestibule to verify it. Yes, I had not been mistaken, it was his cloak. A fashionable cloak, of course. Everything about him—although I could not explain the why and wherefore—I observed with extraordinary attention. I asked if he was visiting and the servant said yes. I passed through the study room, not the drawing room, into the music room. My daughter, Lisa, was sitting with her book, and the nurse was sitting at the table with the little girl spinning a top. The door into the music room was closed, but I could hear the sound of arpeggios and the sound of her voice and his. I listened but could not hear their words. The notes of the piano were played on purpose to drown out their words, perhaps their kisses! My God, what a storm arose in me! The mere thought of the angry beast roused in me fills me with horror. My heart suddenly contracted, stopped, then began to pound like a sledge hammer.

"My chief feeling, as always in an outburst of anger, was pity for myself. 'Before the children! Before the nurse!' I exclaimed inwardly. I must have been terrible to look at because even Lisa looked at me with frightened eyes. 'What is there for me to do?' I asked myself. 'Shall I go in? I can't! God knows what I should do! But I can't go away!' The nurse was looking at me as if she understood my situation. 'But I can't just not go in!' I said to myself and hurriedly flung open the door.

"He was sitting at the piano playing those arpeggios with his long white fingers. She was standing at the other end of the grand piano bending over an opened score. She was the first to see or hear me and she looked up. I don't know whether she was startled and pretended not to be startled or whether she really was not startled—at any rate, she did not show any agitation or even move. She merely blushed, but that was afterward.

" 'I'm so glad you've come. We can't decide what to play next Sunday,' she said in a tone which she would never have used when we were alone. That—and the fact that she said 'we,' connecting herself and him—exasperated me. I silently bowed to him. He pressed my hand and, with a smile which seemed to me derisive, instantly began to explain that he had brought some music for Sunday but that they could not agree what to play: whether something difficult and classical, such as a Beethoven violin sonata, or some easy trifles. All this was so natural and direct that it was impossible to find any fault with it, and yet I was convinced that it was all a falsehood, that they had been planning how to deceive me.

"One of the most torturing conditions for jealous men—and all of us are jealous in our fashionable society—are certain social conventions whereby the greatest and most dangerous proximity is permitted a man and woman. People would simply make themselves ridiculous if they tried to prevent this nearness at dances, between doctors and their female patients, between artists, and especially between musicians. Two people occupy themselves with the noblest of arts—music. A certain proximity is necessary, and there is nothing wrong in it. Only a stupid, jealous husband could find anything wrong in it. But meantime, precisely by means of these very occupations, especially by music, the largest part of the adultery in our society is committed.

"I confused them by the confusion which I myself showed; it was long before I could speak a word. I was like an upturned bottle from which the water will not flow because it is too full. I wanted to heap abuses on him, to drive him away, but I felt that it was my duty to be friendly and cordial to him again, so I was. I pretended that I approved of everything, and once more I felt that strange impulse which compelled me to treat him with a friendliness proportioned to the torment which his presence caused me.

"I told him that I had great confidence in his taste and I advised her to trust his judgment. He stayed just long enough to do away with the disagreeable impression made by my sudden appearance with such an alarmed face and my confused silence; he then left saying that they had now determined what they would play the next day. I was perfectly convinced that, in comparison with what was really occupying them, the question as to what they should play was immaterial.

"I accompanied him with more than ordinary courtesy to the vestibule. How could one fail to treat courteously a man who had come on purpose to disturb my peace of mind and destroy the happiness of a whole family? I pressed his soft white hand with special warmth.

CHAPTER XXII

"That whole day I did not speak to her—I could not. Her presence produced such hatred of her that I feared for my control. At dinner, in the presence of the children, she asked me when I was going away. My duties called me the following week to a meeting of the District Council. I told her when. She asked me if I needed anything for my journey. I did not say anything; I sat in silence at the table, and then silently went to my study. Of late she had stopped coming to my study, especially at that time of day. I was lying down, bitterly angry. Suddenly I heard her steps. The terrible, ugly thought leaped to my brain that she, like Uriah's wife,[10] had already committed the sin and wanted to hide it—that was why she was coming to me! 'Can it be that she is really coming to me?' I asked myself as I heard her approaching. 'If she is coming to me, then it means I am right.' An ineffable hatred of her arose in my soul. Nearer, nearer came her steps. 'Can it be that she is going by into the hall?'

"No, the door creaked and her tall, handsome figure appeared; her face, her eyes expressed timidity and a desire to make up, as I could easily see. I understood the significance of her behavior perfectly. I almost suffocated, so long I held my breath, and continuing to stare at her, I grasped my cigarette case and began to smoke.

" 'Now, how can you? Someone comes to sit with you and you start smoking,' she said. She sat down near me on the divan and leaned against me. I moved away, not to be in contact with her.

" 'I see you're annoyed because I'm going to play on Sunday,' she said.

" 'Not in the least,' I said.

" 'But I see that you are!'

" 'Well, I congratulate you on your insight! I see nothing except that you behave like a coquette. To you all such kinds of vulgarity are pleasant, but to me they are revolting.'

" 'If you're going to abuse me like a carriage driver, I'll go.'

" 'Then, go! But if the honor of your family is not dear to you, neither are you dear to me—the devil take you!—but the honor of the family is—'

" 'What do you mean?'

" 'Get out of my sight! For God's sake, get out!'

"I don't know whether she pretended that she did not understand or really didn't, but she took offense, grew angry, and instead of leaving stood in the middle of the room.

" 'You have become positively unendurable!' she began. 'You have such a disposition that not even an angel could get along with you!' And, as always, trying to wound me as keenly as possible, she reminded me of the way I had treated my sister. (It happened that one time I forgot myself and spoke some harsh words to my sister; she knew about it and that it tormented me.) So she wounded me in that place. 'After that, nothing that you could do would surprise me!' she said.

" 'Yes, insult me, humiliate me, disgrace me, make me out to blame!' I said to myself. Suddenly a terrible anger against her seized me, such as I had never before experienced. For the first time I felt the impulse to express this rage with physical force. I leaped up and moved toward her, but at the instant I became conscious of my anger, and asked myself, 'Is it wise to give way to this impulse?' Immediately the answer came that it was, that this would frighten her; so, instead of withholding my wrath, I began to fan it to greater heat and to rejoice because it grew more and more intense.

" 'Get out of here or I'll kill you!' I screamed, moving toward her and seizing her by the arm. I was aware of raising my voice to a higher pitch, and I must have become terrifying because she became so frightened that she had not the power to go. She merely stammered, 'Vasya! What is it? What is the matter with you?'

" 'Go!' I cried in a still louder tone. 'No one but you can drive me to madness. I won't be responsible for what I may do!'

"Having given free rein to my madness I delighted in it. I wanted to do something extraordinary which would show the high-water mark of my fury. I had a terrible impulse to strike her, to kill her; but I knew that it was out of the question, so—to relieve my anger—I snatched up a paperweight from the table and, shouting, *'Go!'* I flung it to the floor near her. I aimed it carefully so as to strike near her. She left the room but remained standing in the doorway. And then while she was still looking—I did it so that she might see—I began to snatch up from the table various objects—the candlestick, the inkstand—and hurled them all on the floor, still continuing to shout, 'Go! Out of my sight! I won't be responsible for what I may do!'

"She went, and I immediately stopped.

"In an hour the nurse came and told me that my wife was in a state of hysteria. I went to her: she was sobbing and laughing; she could not speak a word and was trembling all over. She was not pretending; she was really ill. Toward morning she grew calm, and we had a reconciliation under the influence of that passion we call love.

"In the morning, after our reconciliation, I confessed to her that I was jealous of Trukhashevsky. She was not in the least confused, and laughed in the most natural manner. So strange to her seemed, as she said, the possibility of being drawn to such a man!

" 'Is it possible that a respectable woman could feel anything for such a man beyond the pleasure which his music might afford? But, if you wish, I am ready not to see him again. Even though all the guests are invited for Sunday, write him I am ill and that will be the end of it. Only one thing makes me indignant, and that is that anyone could imagine, and especially he himself, that he is dangerous. I am too proud to permit myself to think that.'

"And evidently she was not lying. She believed in what she was saying; she hoped by these words to evoke in herself scorn for him and to defend herself from him, but she did not succeed in this. Everything went against her, especially that cursed music.

"Thus the episode ended, and on Sunday the guests gathered and they played together again.

CHAPTER XXIII

"I think it is superfluous to remark that I was very ostentatious. There would not be any living in our general society if it were not for ostentation! Thus, on that Sunday, I took the greatest pains to arrange for our dinner and for the evening musicale. I myself ordered the things for dinner and invited the guests.

"At six o'clock the guests had arrived, and he also, in evening dress with diamond shirt studs of bad taste. He was completely at ease, quickly answered all questions with a smile of sympathy and appreciation—you know what I mean, with that peculiar expression that signifies that everything you say or do is exactly what he expected. I noticed now with special satisfaction everything about him that would give an unfavorable impression, because all this served to calm me and to prove that he stood in my wife's eyes on such a low level that, as she said, she could not possibly descend to it. I did not allow myself to be jealous. In the first place, I had already been through the pangs of that torment and needed rest; in the second place, I wanted to have faith in my wife's assurances, and I did believe in them. But in spite of the fact that I was not jealous, still I was not at ease with either of them, and during the dinner and the first half of the evening before the music began, I kept watching their motions and glances all the time.

"The dinner was like any dinner—dull and conventional. The music began rather early. How well I remember all the details of that evening! I remember how he brought his violin, opened the case, took off the covering which had been embroidered for him by some lady, took out the instrument and began to tune it. I remember how my wife sat with a pretendedly indifferent face under which I saw that she was hiding great uncertainty—the uncertainty caused chiefly by distrust of her own ability—how she took her seat at the grand piano with the same forced look and struck the usual A, which was followed by the pizzicato of the violin and the getting into tune. I remember how they looked at each other, glanced at the audience, and then made some remark. The music began. He sounded the first chords. His face grew grave, stern, and sympathetic, and as he bent his head to listen to the sounds he produced, he placed his fingers cautiously on the strings. The piano replied. And so it began."

Pozdnyshev paused and several times emitted his peculiar sounds. He started to speak again but snuffed through his nose and again paused.

"They played Beethoven's *Kreutzer Sonata*,"[11] he finally went on to say. "Do you know the first Presto? You do know it?" he cried. "Ugh! That sonata is a terrible thing. And especially that movement! Music in general is a terrible thing. I cannot comprehend it. What is music? What does it do? And why does it have the effect it has? They say music has the effect of elevating the soul—rubbish! Nonsense! It has its effect, it has a terrible effect—I am speaking about its effect on me—but not at all of elevating the soul. Its effect is neither to elevate nor to degrade but to excite. How can I explain to to you? Music makes me forget myself, my real situation. It transports me into a state that is not my natural one. Under the influence of music it seems to me that I feel what I do not really feel, that I understand what I do not really understand, that I can do what I can't do. I explain this by the fact that music acts like gaping or laughing: I am not sleepy but I gape, looking at anyone else who is gaping; I have nothing to laugh at, but I laugh when I hear others laugh.

"Music instantaneously transports me into that mental condition in which he who composed it found himself. I blend my soul with his, and with him I am transported from one mood to another. But I cannot tell why this is so. For instance, he who composed the *Kreutzer Sonata*—Beethoven—he knew why he was in that mood. That mood impelled him to do certain things; therefore that mood meant something for him, but it means nothing for me. And that is why music excites and does not bring to any conclusion. When they play a military march, the soldiers move forward under its strains and the music accomplishes something. They play dance music and I dance, and the music accomplishes something. They perform a mass, I take the sacrament; again the music accomplishes its purpose. But in other cases there is only excitement, and it is impossible to tell what to do in this state of mind. And that is why music is so awesome, why it sometimes has such a terrifying effect. In China, music is regulated by government, and this is as it should be. Is it permissible that just anyone at all can hypnotize another person, or many persons, and then do with them what he pleases? And especially if this hypnotizer happens to be the first immoral man that comes along?

"Indeed it is a terrible power to place in anyone's hands. For example, how could anyone play this *Kreutzer Sonata*, the first Presto, in a drawing room before ladies dressed in low-cut gowns? To play that Presto, then to applaud it, and then to eat ices and talk over the last bit of scandal? These things should be played only under certain grave, significant conditions, and only then when certain deeds corresponding to such music are to be accomplished: first play the music and perform that which this music was composed for. But to call forth an energy which is not consonant with the place or the time, and an impulse which does not manifest itself in anything, cannot fail to have a harmful effect. On me, at least, it had a horrible impact. It seemed to me that entirely new impulses, new possibilities, were revealed to me in myself, such as I had never dreamed of before.

" 'This is the way I should live and think—not at all as I have lived and thought hitherto,' seemed to be whispered into my soul. What this new thing was I now knew I could not explain even to myself, but the consciousness of this new state of mind was very delightful. All those faces—his and my wife's among them—presented themselves in a new light.

"After the Allegro they played the beautiful but rather trite and un-original Andante—with its uninspired variations—and the weak Finale. Then at the request of the guests they played other things, first an elegy by Ernst and then various other trifles. All this was very good, but it did not produce on me a hundredth part of the impression which the first did. But all the music had as a background the impression which the first produced.

"I felt gay and happy. I never saw my wife look as she did that evening: her glistening eyes, her dignity and serenity of expression while she was playing, her perfectly melting mood, her tenderly pathetic and blissful smile after they had finished playing. I saw it all, but attributed it to the notion that she was experiencing the same thing I was, that before her, as before me, new and hitherto unexampled feelings were revealed, dimly rising in her consciousness. The evening was a great success and the guests departed.

"Knowing that I was to be going to the district meeting in two days, Trukhashevsky, on bidding me farewell, said he hoped that when he next came to Moscow he would have another pleasant evening like that. From this remark I was able to conclude that he did not deem it possible to visit my house during my absence, and that was agreeable to me. It seemed clear that, since I would not return before his departure, we would not meet again.

"For the first time I shook hands with him with genuine pleasure, and I thanked him for the pleasure he had afforded us. He also bade my wife a final farewell.

"Their farewell seemed to me most natural and proper. Everything was admirable. Both my wife and I were very well satisfied with the evening.

CHAPTER XXIV

"Two days later I started for my district meetings, taking leave of my wife in the happiest and calmest frame of mind.

"In our district there was always a pile of work and a special life, a special little world. For two days I worked ten hours a day in my office. On the third day a letter from my wife was brought to me in the office. I read it at once.

"She wrote about the children, about her uncle, about the nurse, about the things she had bought, and mentioned—as something perfectly commonplace—the fact that Trukhashevsky had called to bring the music he had promised and that he had offered to come to play again but that she had declined.

"I did not remember that he had promised to bring any music. I had supposed that he had taken his final leave at that time, and so this was an unpleasant surprise. But I was so deeply engrossed in business that I could not stop to think further about it; it was not until evening, when I returned to my room, that I reread her letter.

"Besides the fact that Trukhashevsky had called again in my absence, the whole tone of the letter seemed to me unnatural. The frantic beast of jealousy roared in his cage and wanted to break forth. I was afraid of this beast and I shut him up.

" 'What a vile feeling this jealousy is!' I said to myself. 'What can be more natural than what she has written?'

"And I lay on my bed and tried to plan the business to attend to the next day. I never go to sleep very quickly in a new place, but this time I fell asleep almost immediately. But as often happens, I suddenly felt something like an electric shock and started up wide awake. As I woke, I woke with a thought of her, of my carnal love for her, and of Trukhashevsky, and of all that had gone on between him and her. Horror and rage crushed my heart! I tried to reason myself out of it.

" 'What rubbish!' I exclaimed. 'There is not the slightest basis for any such suspicions. And how can I humiliate myself and her by harboring such horrible thoughts? Here is a hired fiddler, with a reputation of being worthless. Could a respectable woman, the mother of a family, *my wife*, suddenly fall a victim to such a man? What an absurdity!'

"That is what I argued on one side, but on the other came these thoughts: 'How could it fail to be so? Why is it not the simplest and most comprehensible thing? Was it not for that I married her? Was it not for that I lived with her? Was it not that which makes me necessary to her? And would not another man, this musician, be likewise necessary to her? He is an unmarried man, healthy—I remember how lustily he crunched the gristle in the cutlet and put the glass of wine to his red lips—he is well-fed, and he is not only without principles but evidently guided by the theory that it is best to take advantage of whatever pleasures present themselves. And between them is the tie of music, the subtle lust of the senses. What can restrain him? She? Yes, but who is she? She is as much a riddle as she has ever been. I don't know her. I know her only as an animal, and nothing can restrain an animal or is likely to.'

"At that instant I recalled their faces that evening after they had played the *Kreutzer Sonata* and while they were performing some passionate piece—I have forgotten what it was—something so sentimental as to seem almost obscene.

" 'How could I have come away?' I asked myself, as I recalled their faces. 'Was it not perfectly evident that the fatal step was taken by them that evening? Was it not evident that from that evening on, not only was there no bar between them, but that both of them—she especially—felt some sense of shame after what had happened to them? I recalled with what a soft blissful smile she wiped away the perspiration from her heated face as I approached the piano. Even then they avoided looking at each other, and only at dinner, when he poured her some water, did they look at each other and smile timidly. I remembered with horror that glance which I had intercepted and that almost imperceptible smile.

" 'Yes, the fatal step has been taken,' said a voice within me. Instantly another voice seemed to say quite the contrary. 'You are crazy; this cannot be!'

"It was painful for me to lie there in the darkness. I lit a match, and then it seemed to me terrible to be in that little room with its yellow wallpaper. I began to smoke a cigarette, and, as is always the case when one turns round in the same circle of irresolvable contradictions, I smoked—smoked one cigarette after another, for the purpose of befogging my mind and not seeing all the contradictions.

"I did not sleep all night, and at five o'clock, having made up my mind that I could remain no longer in such a state of tension but would instantly go back, I got up, wakened the porter and sent him after horses. I sent a note to the Council meeting that I had been called back to Moscow on extraordinary business and therefore begged them to let another member take my place. At eight o'clock I took my seat in the carriage and started."

CHAPTER XXV

The conductor came through the train, and noticing that our candle was almost burned out, he extinguished it instead of putting in another. It was beginning to grow light. Pozdnyshev stopped speaking and sighed heavily all the time the conductor was in the carriage. He proceeded with his story only when the conductor had gone. The only sound we could hear in the semi-darkness of the carriage was the rattle of the windows and regular snore of the clerk. In the dim light of dawn I could not make out Pozdnyshev's face clearly, but I could hear his passionate voice growing ever more and more excited.

"I had to travel twenty-five miles by horse and eight hours by rail. It was splendid traveling with horses. It was frosty autumnal weather with a brilliant sun—you know, that kind of weather when the tires leave their print on the slippery road. The roads were smooth, the light was dazzling, and the air was exhilarating. Yes, it was good traveling by horse and carriage. As soon as it grew light, and I was fairly on my way, my heart felt lighter.

"As I looked at the horses, at the fields, at the persons I met, I forgot my errand. It sometimes seemed to me that I was simply out for a drive, and that there was nothing whatever to stir me so. And I felt particularly happy at thus forgetting myself. If by chance it occurred to me where I was bound, I said to myself: 'Wait and see what will be. Don't think about it now.'

"About halfway an event happened which delayed me and tended to distract my attention still more: the carriage broke down and it was necessary to mend it. This breakdown had great importance because it caused me to reach Moscow at midnight instead of at five o'clock (as I had expected) and home at one o'clock (for I missed the express and was obliged to take a local train). The mending of the carriage, the settlement of the bill, tea at an inn, the conversation with the innkeeper—all this served to divert me more and more. By twilight everything was ready and I was on my way once more; during the evening it was still more pleasant than traveling by day. There was a young moon, a slight touch of frost; the roads were still excellent, and so were the horses; the driver was jolly, and so I traveled on and enjoyed myself, scarcely thinking at all of what was awaiting me. Or perhaps I enjoyed myself especially because I knew what was awaiting me and I was having my last taste of the joys of life.

"But this calm state of mind, the power of controlling my feelings, came to an end as soon as I stopped traveling with the horses. As soon as I entered the railroad carriage an entirely different state of things began. This eight-hour journey by rail was horrible to me, and I shall never forget it as long as I live. Either because as soon as I entered the carriage I vividly imagined myself as having already reached the end, or because railroad travel has an exciting effect on people—in any case, as soon as I took my seat I no longer had control over my imagination, which ceaselessly, with extraordinary vividness, began to bring up before me pictures kindling my jealousy. One after another they arose and always to the same effect: what had taken place during my absence and how she had deceived me! I was on fire with indignation, wrath, and fury, caused by my humiliation, as I contemplated these pictures. I could not tear myself away from them, could not help gazing at them, could not rub them out, could not help evoking them. And the more I contemplated these imaginary pictures the more I was convinced of their reality. The vividness with which these pictures presented themselves seemed to serve as a proof of the actuality of all that I imagined. A kind of a devil, completely against my will, suggested and stimulated the most horrible suggestions. A conversation I once had with Trukhashevsky's brother occurred to me, and with a sort of pleasure I lacerated my heart with this conversation, applying it to Trukhashevsky and my wife.

"It had taken place long before, but it now came back clearly to me. I remembered that Trukhashevsky's brother, in reply to a question of whether he ever went to certain houses, stated that no decent man would ever go to such places where there was danger of contracting disease, that it was vile and disgusting, and that one could always find some society woman to serve his purpose. And now here was his brother—and he had found my wife!

" 'To be sure, she is no longer young; she has a tooth missing on one side of her mouth; her face is somewhat puffy,' I said, trying to look from his standpoint. 'But what difference does that make? One must take what one can get. Yes, he is conferring a favor on her to take her as his mistress,' I said to myself. 'Then besides, there is no danger with her. No, it is impossible!' I exclaimed in horror. 'There is no possibility of it, not the least, and there is not the slightest basis for any such conjectures. Has she not told me that to her it was a humiliating thought that I could be jealous of him? Yes, but she is a liar, always a liar!' I thought.

"There were only two passengers in my carriage—an old woman and her husband, both very silent. They got out at the first stop, and I was alone. I was like a raging beast in a cage; now I would jump up and rush to the window, then I would walk back and forth through the aisle trying to make the train go faster. But the carriage with all its seats and its windowpanes rattled along just exactly as ours is doing now."

Pozdnyshev sprang to his feet, took a few steps and then sat down again.

"Oh, I hate, I hate these railroad carriages—they fill me with complete horror—yes, I hate them deeply," he went on. "I said to myself, 'I must think of something else; let me think of the landlord of the inn where I took tea.' Then before my eyes would arise the long-bearded innkeeper and his grandson, a boy about as old as my Vasya.

" 'My Vasya! He will see a musician kissing his mother! What will happen to his poor soul at the sight? But what will she care? She is in love!'

"And again would arise the same visions! 'No, no! I will think about the inspection of the hospital . . . Yesterday that sick man complained of the doctor . . . A doctor with mustaches just like Trukhashevsky's . . . And how brazen he—they both deceived me, when he said that he was going away!' And again it would begin: everything I thought of had some connection with them! I suffered. My chief suffering lay in my ignorance, in the uncertainty of it all, in my question whether I ought to love her or hate her. These sufferings were so intense that I remember I was tempted to go out on the track and throw myself under the train and so end it. Then, at least, there would be no further doubt. The one thing that prevented me from doing so was my self-pity, which was the immediate source of my hatred of her. I had a strange feeling of hatred toward him and a full awareness of the humiliation in his victory. Toward her my hatred was boundless.

" 'It is impossible to put an end to myself and to leave her behind. I must do something to make her suffer, so that she may appreciate that I have suffered,' I said to myself.

"I got out at every one of the stations in order to divert my mind. At one station I noticed that people were drinking in the restaurant, so I immediately fortified myself with vodka. Next to me stood a Jew, who was also drinking. He spoke to me and, so that I might not be alone in my carriage, I went with him into his third-class compartment. It was filthy and full of smoke and littered with the husks of seeds. I sat down next to him, and he went on chattering and telling stories. I could hear him and yet I did not hear what he said, for I kept thinking of my own affairs. He noticed this and tried to attract my attention. I got up and went back to my own carriage.

" 'I must think it all over again,' I said to myself, 'whether what I think is true and whether there is any foundation for my anguish.' I sat down, trying to think it over calmly, but instantly the same tumult of thought began. In place of argument, pictures and figments of the imagination!

" 'How often have I tortured myself so,' I said to myself, for I re-membered similar paroxysms of jealousy in times gone by, 'and then there was no ground for them. And so now, possibly—no, probably—I will find her calmly sleeping. She will wake up and be glad to see me, and I will know both from her words and her looks that nothing has taken place and that my suspicions were groundless. Oh! How won-derful that would be!'

" 'But no, this has been so too frequently and now it will be so no longer,' said some inner voice, and once more it would begin anew. What a punishment was here! I would not take a young man to a syphilitic hospital to cure him of his passion for women, but into my own soul, to give him a glimpse of the fiends that were rending it. It was horrible! I claimed an absolute right to her body just as if it had been my own body; at the same time I was aware that I could not con-trol that body of hers, that it was not mine, that she had the power to dispose of it as she chose, and that she did not choose to dispose of it as I wished. I could not do anything to her or to him! He, like Vanka the cellarer before he was hanged, will sing a song of how he had kissed her on her sugary lips and the like. He would have the best of me. And with her I could do even less! If she had not yet done anything out of the way, but had it in mind to—and I know that she did—the case is still worse. It would be better to have it done with, so as to have this uncertainty settled.

"I could not tell what I really wanted. I wanted her not to desire what she could not help desiring. This was absolute madness!

CHAPTER XXVI

"At the next to the last station, when the conductor came along to take the tickets, I picked up my belongings and went out on the platform. The realization of what was about to take place increased my agitation. I became cold, and my jaws trembled so that my teeth chattered. Mechanically I followed the crowd out of the station, engaged a driver, took my seat in his cab, and we drove away. As I drove along, glancing at the occasional pedestrians, at the watchmen and the shadows cast by the street lamps and my cab, now in front and now behind, my mind seemed a blank. By the time we had driven half a mile from the station my feet became cold; I remembered that I had removed my woolen stockings in the train and put them in my suitcase. Where was it? Had I brought it with me? Yes, I had. Where was my wicker case? Then I realized that I had entirely forgotten about my baggage, but, while I was thinking about it, I found my receipt and decided that it was not worth while returning for it, so I drove home.

"In spite of my efforts I can never remember to this day what my state of mind was at that time—what I thought, what I wanted. I only remember that I knew something terrible and very vital in my life was going to happen. Whether this important event proceeded from the fact that I thought so or because I had foreboded it, I do not know. Perhaps after what happened subsequently, all the preceding moments have taken on a gloomy shade in my recollection.

"I reached the doorstep. It was one o'clock. Several drivers waiting for fares were standing in front of the door in the light cast by the windows. The lighted windows were in our apartment, in the music room and the drawing room. I made no attempt to figure out myself why our windows were still lighted so late at night. Expectant of something dreadful, I went up the steps and rang the bell. Egor, the butler, a good-natured, zealous, but extremely stupid fellow, answered it. The first thing that struck my eyes in the vestibule was a cloak hanging on a peg with other outside garments. I ought to have been surprised but I was not—it was what I expected. 'It is true,' I said to myself.

"When I asked Egor who was there and he said Trukhashevsky, I asked, 'Is there anyone else with them?' And he said, 'No one.'

"I remember that in his reply there was an intonation, as if he felt he was pleasing me in dispelling my apprehension that anyone else was there.

" 'It is true, it is true!' I seemed to say to myself.

" 'The children?'

" 'Thank God, they are well. They have been asleep for several hours.'

"I could not breathe freely, nor could I prevent the trembling of my jaw. 'Yes, of course, it is not as I thought it might be; whereas formerly I imagined some misfortune and yet found everything all right, as usual, now it was not usual, now it was altogether what I had imagined and fancied that I only imagined, but it was now real. It was all . . .'

"I almost began to sob, but instantly a fiend suggested: 'Shed tears! Be sentimental! But they will part quietly; there will be no proof; you will forever be in doubt and torment.'

"Thereupon my self-pity vanished. In its place came a strange feeling of anticipation that my torture was now at an end, that I could punish her, could get rid of her—that I could give free rein to my wrath. And that I did—I became a beast, fierce and sly.

" 'No matter, no matter,' I said to Egor, who was about to go into the drawing room. 'Take care of this instead: get a driver and go as quickly as you can to the station for my luggage; here is the receipt. Off with you!'

"He went into the corridor to get his overcoat. Fearing that he might warn them, I accompanied him to his little room and waited till he had got his things on. In the drawing room, just through the wall, I could hear the sound of voices and the clatter of knives and dishes. They were eating and had not heard the bell.

" 'If only no one leaves the room now,' I thought to myself.

"Egor put on his overcoat trimmed with lamb's wool. I let him out and shut the door behind him. I felt a sense of dread at the idea of being left alone and of having to act instantly.

"I did not know how as yet. All I knew was that all was ended, that there could be no longer any doubt as to her guilt, that I would soon punish her and put an end to my relations with her.

"Hitherto I had been troubled with vacillation. I had said to myself: 'Maybe it is not so, maybe you are mistaken.' Now this was at an end. Everything was now irrevocably decided. Secretly! Alone with him! At night! This proved perfect disregard of everything! Or something even worse! Such audacity, such insolence in crime was deliberately adopted in order that its very insolence might serve as a proof of innocence! All was clear, there could be no doubt! I was afraid of only one thing—that they might escape, might invent some new lie to deprive me of clear proof and of the possibility of convincing myself. So as to catch them as promptly as possible I went, not through the drawing room, but through the corridor and the nursery, on my tiptoes, into the music room where they were sitting.

"In the first nursery room the boys were sound asleep. In the second nursery room the nurse stirred and was on the point of waking up; I imagined to myself what she would think if she knew it all. And then such a feeling of self-pity came over me at this thought that I could not restrain my tears. In order not to wake the children I ran out, on tiptoes, into the corridor and into my own room, flung myself down on my divan, and sobbed.

" 'I, an upright man . . . I, the son of my own parents . . . I, who have dreamed all my life of the delights of domestic happiness . . . I, a husband who has never been unfaithful to my wife . . . ! And here she, the mother of five children, embracing a musician because he has red lips!

" 'No, she is not human! She is a bitch, a vile bitch! Next to the room where her children sleep, whom, all her life, she has pretended to love! And to write me what she wrote! And so brazenly to throw herself into my arms! And how do I know that this same sort of thing has not been taking place all the time? Who knows but the children whom I have always supposed to be mine may not have some servant for their father?

" 'And if I had come home tomorrow she would have met me with her hair becomingly done up and with her graceful, indolent movements'—all the time I seemed to see her fascinating, abhorrent face—'and this wild beast of jealousy would have taken his position forever in my heart and torn it. What will the nurse think . . . and Egor . . . and poor little Lisa? She already has her suspicions. This brazen impudence! This falsehood! And this animal sensuality which I know so well!' I said to myself.

"I tried to get up but could not. My heart throbbed so that I could not stand on my legs.

" 'God! I will die of a stroke. She will have killed me. That is just what she wants! What would it be to her to kill me? Indeed, it would be quite too advantageous, and I will not give her that satisfaction! Yes, here I sit and there they eat and talk together, and . . .

" 'Yes, in spite of the fact that she is no longer in her early youth, he will not despise her. She is not bad-looking, and, what is the main thing, she is not dangerous for his precious health. Why, then, have I not strangled her already?' I asked myself, recalling that moment a week before when I drove her out of my study and then smashed things. I had a vivid remembrance of the state of mind in which I was then. I not only had the remembrance, but I felt the same necessity of striking, of destroying, as I had felt before. I remember how I wanted to do something, how all considerations except those that were necessary for action vanished from my mind. I was like a wild animal, or, rather, like a man under the influence of physical excitement in time of danger, when he acts definitely, deliberately, without losing a single instant, all the time with a single object in view.

"First I took off my boots. Then, in my stocking feet, I went to the wall where some weapons and daggers were hung over the divan. I took down a curved Damascus dagger which had never been used and was very keen. I drew it out of its sheath. I remember the sheath slipped down behind the divan, and I remember I said to myself, 'I must find it afterward or else it will get lost.' Then I took off my overcoat, which I had all the time been wearing, and, walking quietly along in my stockings, I went *there*.

CHAPTER XXVII

"I suddenly threw open the door. I remember the expression on both of their faces. I remember that expression because it gave me a tormenting pleasure—it was an expression of complete horror! That was the very thing I needed! I shall never forget the expression of despairing horror which came into their faces the first second they saw me. He was seated at the table, but when he saw me or heard me he leaped to his feet and stood with his back against the sideboard. His face bore the unmistakable expression of terror. On her face also was an expression of terror, but there was something else blended with it. If it had not been for that something else, maybe what happened would not have happened. But in the expression of her face there was, or so there seemed to me at the first instant, a look of disappointment, of annoyance that her pleasure in his love and her enjoyment with him were interrupted. It was as if she wanted nothing else than to be left undisturbed in her present happiness. These expressions lingered but a moment on their faces. The look of terror on his face at once grew into a look which asked the question: 'Is it possible to lie out of this or not? If it is possible, now is the time to begin. If not, then something else must be done—but what?'

"He looked questioningly at her. On her face the expression of annoyance and disappointment changed, it seemed to me, when she looked at him, into one of solicitude for him.

"I stood for a moment on the threshold, the dagger behind my back.

"During that second he smiled and, in a voice so indifferent that it was ludicrous, he began: 'We have been having some music . . .'

" 'Why! I was not expecting you . . .' she began at the same time, adopting his tone.

"But neither he nor she finished their sentences. The very same madness I had experienced a week before took possession of me! Once more I felt the necessity of destroying something, of using violence! Once more I sensed the ecstasy of madness and I yielded to it! Neither finished what they were saying. The something else which terrified him began. It swept away instantaneously all that they had to say.

"I threw myself on her, still concealing the dagger in order that he might not prevent me from striking her in the side under the breast! I had chosen that spot at the very beginning. The instant I threw myself on her he saw my intent and, with an action I never expected from him, he seized me by the arm and cried: 'Think what you . . . Help!'

"I wrenched away my arm and without saying a word rushed at him. His eyes met mine. He suddenly turned as pale as a sheet, even to the lips. His eyes glittered with a peculiar light. Suddenly he slipped under the piano and darted out the door. I started to rush after him, but I was held back by a pull on my left arm. It was she! I tried to break away. She clung all the more heavily to my arm and would not let me go. This unexpected hindrance—the weight of her, her touch which was repulsive to me—still further inflamed my anger! I was conscious of being in a complete frenzy and that I ought to be terrifying—and I exulted in it. I drew back my left arm with all my might and struck her full in the face with my elbow. She screamed and let go my arm. I started to chase him, but remembered that it would be ridiculous for a man to chase his wife's lover in his stockings. I did not want to be ridiculous; I wanted to be fearful.

"Notwithstanding the terrible frenzy in which I found myself, I never for an instant forgot the impression I might produce on others, and this impression, to a certain degree, governed me. I came back to her. She had fallen on a couch, and with her hand held up to her eyes, which I had bruised, was looking at me, her enemy, as a rat might when the trap in which it had been caught is picked up. I could see nothing else in her face except terror and hatred—precisely the same which love for another would evoke. Possibly I would have restrained myself and not done what I did if she had held her tongue. But she suddenly began to speak, and she seized my hand which held the dagger: 'Come to your senses! What are you going to do? What is the matter with you? There has been nothing—no harm, I swear it!'

"I would have still delayed, but these last words—from which I drew exactly the opposite conclusion, that is, that my worst fears were realized—required an answer. And the answer had to correspond to the fury I now felt, which had risen in a crescendo and was now unalterably reaching its climax. Madness also has its laws!

"'Don't lie, you bitch!' I cried, and with my left hand I seized her by the arm, but she tore herself away. Then, still clutching the dagger, I grasped her by the throat, pressed her over backward and began to strangle her. What a muscular throat she had! She grasped my hands, pulling them away from her throat, and I, as if I had been waiting for this opportunity, struck her with the dagger deep in the side under the ribs.

"When men say that in an attack of madness they don't remember what they did, it is all false, all nonsense. I remember every detail, and not for one second did I fail to remember. The more violently I kindled within me the flames of my madness, the more brightly burned the light of consciousness, so that I could not fail to see all that I did. I knew every second what I was doing. I cannot say that I knew in advance what I was going to do, but at the instant I did anything, and perhaps a little before, I knew what I was up to—as if for the sake of being able to repent, of being able to say to myself, 'I might have stopped.' I knew that I struck below the ribs and that the dagger would penetrate. At the moment I was doing this, I knew that I was doing something, something awful, something I had never done before, something which would have awful consequences. But this consciousness flashed through my mind like lightning and was instantly followed by the deed. The deed made itself real with unexampled clearness. I felt, I remember, the momentary resistance of her corset and of something else, and then the sinking of the blade into the soft parts of her body. She seized the dagger with her hands, cutting them, but she could not stop me.

"Afterward, in the prison, while a moral revolution was working itself out in me, I thought much about that moment—what I might have done—and I thought it all over. I remember that a second, only a second, before the deed was accomplished, I had the terrible realization that I was killing a woman—a defenseless woman—my wife. I recall the horror of this awareness, and therefore I conclude—and indeed I dimly remember—that, having plunged the dagger in, I immediately withdrew it with the impulse to remedy what I had done. I stood motionless for a second, waiting to see what would happen—and whether I might undo what I had done.

"She rose to her feet, and shrieked: 'Nurse, he has killed me!'

"The nurse had heard the disturbance and was already at the door. I was still standing, expectant and uncertain. At that instant the blood gushed from under her corset. Only then did I realize it was impossible to remedy it. I knew at once that it was not necessary, that I myself did not wish to have it remedied, that I had done the very thing I was in duty bound to do. She fell and the nurse, crying, 'Dear God!' rushed to her. I flung the dagger down and ran from the room.

" 'I must not get excited; I must know what I am doing,' I said to myself, looking neither at her nor at the nurse. The nurse screamed, and called to the maid. I went along the corridor, passed the maid, and went to my room.

" 'What must I do now?' I asked myself. I made up my mind. As soon as I reached my study I went directly to the wall and took down a revolver. It was loaded. I laid it on the table. I picked up the sheath from behind the divan. I sat down on the divan.

"I sat long in that way. My mind was without a thought, without a recollection. I heard some commotion *there*. I heard someone arrive, then someone else. Then I heard and saw Egor bringing my luggage into my study. As if that would be useful to anyone now!

" 'Have you heard what has happened?' I asked. 'Tell the porter to call the police!'

"He said nothing, but went out. I got up, closed the door, got my cigarettes and matches, and began to smoke. I had not finished smoking my cigarette before drowsiness seized me and overcame me. I must have slept two hours. I remember I dreamed that she and I were friends, that we had quarreled but had made up, that some trifle had stood in our way but still we were friends.

"A knock on the door awakened me.

" 'It is the police,' I thought as I woke. 'I must have killed her! But maybe it is she herself and nothing has happened.'

"The knocking at the door was repeated. I did not answer, but kept trying to decide the question. 'Had all that really taken place or not?' Yes, it had. I remembered the resistance of the corset and the sinking of the dagger, and a cold chill ran down my back. 'Yes, it is true. Yes, now I must have my turn,' I said to myself. But though I said this I knew I would not kill myself. Nevertheless, I got up and once more took the revolver into my hand. But, strange as it may seem, I remember that many times before I had been near suicide—as, for instance, that very day on the railroad train—and it had seemed to me very easy, for by that I could fill her with consternation.

"Now I could not kill myself or think of such a thing. 'Why should I do it?' I asked myself, and there was no answer.

"The knocking continued at the door.

" 'Yes, first I must find out who is knocking. I shall have time enough afterward . . .'

"I laid the revolver down and covered it with a newspaper. I went to the door and drew back the bolt. It was my wife's sister, a good but stupid widow.

" 'Vasya, what does this mean?' she asked, and her ever-ready tears began to gush forth.

" 'What do you want?' I asked harshly. I saw that this was entirely unnecessary and that I had no reason to be gruff with her, but I could not adopt any other tone.

" 'Vasya, she is dying! Ivan Zakharych says so!'

"Ivan Zakharych was her doctor, her adviser.

" 'Is he here?' I asked, and all my rage against her flamed up once more. 'Well, suppose she is!'

" 'Vasya, go to her! Oh, how horrible this is!' she exclaimed.

" 'Must I go to her?' I wondered. Then I decided that I must go, that probably when a husband had killed his wife as I had, he must always go to her, that it was the proper thing to do.

" 'If it is always done, then I must surely go,' I said to myself. 'Yes, if it is necessary to, I shall; I can still kill myself,' I reasoned in regard to my intention of blowing my brains out, and I followed her.

" 'Now there will be phrases and grimaces, but I will not let them affect me,' I said to myself.

" 'Wait,' I said to her sister. 'It is stupid to go without my boots. Let me at least put on my slippers.'

CHAPTER XXVIII

"Another remarkable thing: once more as I left my room and went through the familiar rooms, once more arose the hope that nothing had taken place, but the odor of the vile medical appliances, iodoform, carbolic acid, struck my senses.

"Yes, all was a reality. As I went through, past the nursery, I caught sight of little Lisa. She looked at me, frightened. It seemed to me then that all five of the children were there and that all of them were looking at me.

"I went to the door. The chambermaid opened it from the inside and went out. The first thing that struck my eyes was her light gray gown lying on a chair and all discolored with blood. She was lying on our double bed, on my side of it—it was easier of access on that side, and her knees were raised. She was placed in a very sloping position on pillows alone, with her bed jacket unbuttoned. Something had been placed over the wound. The room was full of the oppressive odor of iodoform. I was struck by her swollen and bruised face. It was the effect of the blow that I had given her with my elbow when she was trying to hold me back. Her beauty had all vanished. She was repulsive. I paused in the doorway.

" 'Go to her, go,' said her sister.

" 'Yes, she probably wants to confess to me,' I thought. 'Shall I forgive her? Yes, she is dying and it is permissible to forgive her,' I thought, striving to be magnanimous.

"I went close to her. With difficulty she raised her eyes to me—one of them was blackened—and she said with difficulty, with pauses between the words: 'You have had your way . . . you have killed me.'

"And in her face, through her physical suffering and even the nearness of death, could be seen the old expression of cold animal hatred I knew so well.

" 'The children . . . anyway . . . you shall not have . . . She'—indicating her sister—'will take them.'

"As to the principal thing for me—her guilt, her unfaithfulness—she did not consider it worth while to say a word!

" 'Yes . . . delight yourself in what you have done,' she said, glancing at the door and sobbing. In the doorway stood her sister with the children. 'Oh, what have you done?'

"I looked at the children, at her bruised and discolored face, and for the first time forgot myself, my rights, my pride. For the first time I recognized the human being in her. And so petty seemed all that had offended me, all my jealousy, and so significant the deed I had done, that I had the impulse to bow down to her hand and to say, 'Forgive me,' but I had not the courage.

"She remained silent, closing her eyes, too weak to speak further. Her mutilated face was distorted with a frown. She feebly pushed me away.

" 'Why has all this happened? Why?'

" 'Forgive me,' I cried.

" 'Forgive? What nonsense! If only I could live!' she cried, raising herself up. Her deliriously flashing eyes were fastened on me. 'Yes, you have had your way. I hate you. Oh!' she screamed, evidently out of her head, evidently afraid of something. 'Shoot! I am not afraid . . . Only kill us all . . . ! He has gone . . . ! He has gone!'

"The delirium continued to the very end. She did not recognize anyone. On the same day, at noon, she died. Before that, at eight o'clock in the morning, I was arrested and taken to prison. And there, while I was confined for eleven months waiting for my trial, I had a chance to meditate on myself and my past life, and I came to understand it. On the third day I began to comprehend. On the third day they took me *there.*"

He wanted to say something more, but not having the strength to hold back his sobs, he paused. Collecting his strength, he continued.

"I began to understand only when I beheld her in her coffin." He sobbed, but immediately continued. "Only when I beheld her dead face did I realize what I had done. I realized that I—I—had killed her, that it was through me that she, who had been living, moving, warm, was now motionless, waxlike, and cold, and that there was no way of ever again making it right—never, never again! He who has not lived through this cannot understand! Oh! Oh! Oh!" he cried several times and said no more.

We sat a long time in silence. He sobbed and trembled before me. His face became pinched and long; his mouth widened.

"Yes," he said suddenly, "if I had known what I know now, everything would have been altogether different. I would not have married her for . . . I would not have married at all."

Again, there was a long silence. He turned from me, saying, "Excuse me . . ." and lay down on the seat, covering himself with his blanket.

At the station where I was to leave the train—it was eight o'clock in the morning—I went near him to say good-bye. Either he was asleep or he was pretending to be asleep, for he did not move. I touched his hand. He lifted the blanket from his face; it was now plain that he had not really been asleep.

"Good-bye," I said, offering him my hand. He took it and almost smiled, but so piteously that I felt like weeping.

"Yes, good-bye . . . forgive me," he said, repeating the very words with which he had closed his story.[12]

SEQUEL TO THE KREUTZER SONATA[1]

With reference to the subject treated of in my story, "The Kreutzer Sonata," I have received, and am still receiving, many letters from strangers who ask me to explain my opinion clearly and simply. I will do my best to meet their wish, *i.e.,* briefly to express the essence of what I wished that story to convey, and the conclusions which may, I think, be drawn from it.

———

First. I wished to say that a firm conviction (supported by false science) has established itself among all classes of our society, to the effect that sexual intercourse is necessary for health, and that marriage not being always possible, sexual intercourse without marriage, and binding the man to nothing beyond a mere money payment, is quite natural and a thing to be encouraged. This conviction has become so general and so firm that parents, acting on the advice of doctors, arrange opportunities of vice for their children, and governments (which should not exist unless they care for the moral well-being of their citizens) organize vice. That is to say, they organize a whole class of women who have to perish body and soul to satisfy the alleged needs of men. And unmarried people addict themselves to vice with quiet consciences.

And I wished to say that this is wrong. It cannot be necessary to destroy some people, body and soul, for the health of others, any more than it can be necessary for some people to drink the blood of others in order to be healthy.

The deduction which seems to me naturally to follow from the above, is that we should not yield to this error and fraud. And in order not to yield, it is necessary, first of all, not to give credence to immoral doctrines, no matter on what pseudo-sciences they may rest for support. Secondly, we must realize that it is a breach of the simplest demands of morality to enter into sexual intercourse in which people either free themselves from the possible consequences of the act, *i.e.* from the children who may be born, or leave the whole burden to the mother, or take precautions to prevent the birth of children. It is a meanness, and young people who do not wish to be mean should not do it.

To be able to abstain they should lead a natural life: not drink, nor eat meat, nor overeat, nor avoid labor—exhausting labor, not mere gymnastics, or other play. But besides this they should not, even in thought, admit the possibility of connection with strange women, any more than they would with their mothers, sisters, near relations, or with the wives of their friends. Any man can find hundreds of examples around him showing that continence is possible, and less dangerous and less harmful to health than incontinence. That is the first thing.

Second. In all classes of our society conjugal infidelity has become very common. And this is so because sexual intercourse is regarded not only as a pleasure, and as necessary to health, but as being something poetic and elevated, and a blessing to life.

And I think such conduct is wrong, and the deduction to be made is that it should not be indulged in.

And in order not to indulge in it, it is necessary that this way of regarding sexual love should be changed. Men and women should be educated at home and by public opinion, both before and after marriage, not as now to consider being in love and the sexual affection connected therewith as a poetic and elevated condition, but as being an animal condition, degrading to man. And an infringement of the marriage promise of faithfulness should be held by public opinion to be at least as shameful as the infringement of a monetary obligation, or as a commercial fraud. And it should not be extolled in novels, verses, songs, and operas, as is now commonly done. That is the second thing.

Third. Again, as a consequence of the false importance attached to sexual love, the birth of children in our society has lost its meaning. Instead of being the object and justification of conjugal relations, it is now a hindrance to the pleasant continuation of amorous intercourse. And, therefore, both outside marriage and among married people (on the advice of the servants of medical science), the use of means to prevent the woman from conceiving children has spread, and people continue conjugal intercourse during the months when the woman is bearing and nursing the child. This used not to be done formerly, and it is not done now in the patriarchal peasant families.

And I think that such conduct is wrong.

It is bad to use means to prevent the birth of children, both because so doing frees people from the cares and troubles caused by children, which should serve to redeem sexual love, and also because it comes very near to what is most revolting to our conscience—murder. And incontinence during pregnancy and nursing is bad, because it wastes the woman's bodily, and especially her spiritual, strength.

The deduction from this is, that these things should not be done. And in order not to do them it should be understood that continence, which is a necessary condition of man's self-respect when he is unmarried, is even more necessary in the married state. That is the third thing.

Fourth. In our society children are considered either an unfortunate accident, or a hindrance to enjoyment, or (when a preconcerted number are produced) as a sort of delectation. And, in accordance with such a view, the children are not educated to face the problems of human life which await them, as beings endowed with reason and love, but they are merely treated with an eye to the enjoyment they can afford to their parents. Consequently, human children are brought up like the young of animals; the chief care of the parents not being to prepare them for an activity worthy of men, but to feed them as well as possible, to increase their stature, and to make them clean, white, plump, and handsome. In all this, the parents are supported by the pseudo-science of medicine. And if things are done differently among the lower classes, this results merely from their lack of means. The view held is the same in all classes. And in pampered children, as in all overfed animals, an irresistible sensuality shows itself at an abnormally early age, and is the cause of terrible suffering before maturity. Apparel, reading, performances, music, dances, rich food, and all the surroundings of their life, from the pictures on boxes of sweets to novels and stories and poems, increase the sensuality; and the result is that sexual vices and diseases become customary among children of both sexes, and often retain their hold after maturity is reached.

And I think this is wrong. And the deduction to be made is, that human children should not be educated like animals, but that other things should be aimed at in the bringing up of children besides a handsome, pampered body. That is the fourth thing.

Fifth. In our society, where the falling in love of young men and women, which after all has sexual love at its root, is considered poetical and is extolled as the highest aim of human effort (as witness all the art and poetry of our society), young people devote the best time of their life,—the men to spying out, tracking, and obtaining possession of the most desirable objects of love, whether in amours or in marriage; and the women and girls to trapping and luring men into amours or marriages.

And thus people's best strength is spent in efforts that are not only unproductive, but harmful. Most of the senseless luxury of our lives results from this. From this comes the idleness of men and the shamelessness of women, who do not disdain to expose parts of their body that excite desire, in obedience to fashions admittedly borrowed from notoriously depraved women.

And I believe that this is wrong.

It is wrong because the aim—union with the object of one's love, with or without marriage, however it may be poeticized—is an aim unworthy of man, just as the aim of obtaining for oneself delicate and plentiful food is unworthy of man, though considered by many as the supreme aim of life.

The deduction to be made is, that we must cease to think that physical love is something particularly elevated. We must understand that no aim that we consider worthy of man—whether it be the service of humanity, of one's country, of science, or of art (let alone the service of God)—is ever reached by means of union with the object of one's love (whether with or without a marriage rite). On the contrary, being in love, and union with the beloved object, never makes it easier to gain any end worthy of man, but always makes it more difficult.

That is the fifth consideration.

———

That is essentially what I wished to express, and thought I had expressed, in my story. And it seemed to me that the remedy for the evils referred to in these propositions might be discussed, but that it was impossible not to agree with the propositions themselves. This seemed to me so: first, because these propositions quite coincide with what we know of the progress of humanity, which is always proceeding from dissoluteness toward more and more of chastity, and coincide also with the moral consciousness of society,—with our consciences, which always condemn dissoluteness and esteem chastity. Secondly, because these propositions are nothing more than inevitable deductions from the teaching of the Gospels, which we profess, or at least (even if unconsciously) acknowledge to be the basis of our conceptions of morality.

But I was mistaken.

No one, indeed, directly contradicted the positions that it is wrong to be vicious, either before marriage or after a marriage ceremony, that it is wrong artificially to prevent childbirth, that children should not be made playthings of, and that amorous union should not be placed above all other considerations. In brief, no one denied that chastity is better than dissoluteness. But people say: "If it is better not to marry, evidently we should do what is better. But if all men do so, the human race will cease, and it cannot be an ideal for humanity to destroy itself." The extinction of the race, however, is not a new idea. It is an article of faith among religious people, and to scientists it is an inevitable deduction from observation of the cooling of the sun. Leaving all that aside, however, the above rejoinder rests on a great, widely diffused, and ancient misunderstanding. It is said: "If people act up to the ideal of complete chastity, they will be exterminated; therefore, the ideal is false." But, intentionally or unintentionally, those who say this confuse two different things—a precept and an ideal.

Chastity is not a precept, or a rule, but an ideal. And an ideal is only then an *ideal*, when its accomplishment is possible only in *idea*, in thought; and when it appears attainable only in infinity, when, therefore, the possibility of approaching it is endless. If the ideal could be attained now, or if we could even imagine its accomplishment, it would cease to be an ideal.

Such is Christ's ideal—the establishment of the kingdom of God on earth; an ideal already foretold by the prophets who spoke of a time when all men shall be taught of God, and shall beat their swords into plowshares and their spears into pruning-hooks,[2] when the lions shall lie down with the lambs,[3] and all beings shall be united by love. The whole meaning of man's life lies in progress toward that ideal. And, therefore, the striving toward the Christian ideal in its entirety, and toward chastity as one of its conditions, is far from rendering life impossible. On the contrary, the absence of this ideal would destroy progress and thus render real life impossible.

The argument that the human race will cease if men strive resolutely toward chastity, is like the argument sometimes adduced, that the human race will perish if men strive resolutely to learn to love their friends, their enemies, and all that lives, instead of continuing the struggle for existence. Such arguments proceed from not understanding that there are two different methods of moral guidance. As there are two ways of directing a traveler, so there are two ways of supplying moral guidance to a man seeking after truth. One way is to tell the man of things he will meet on his road and by which he can shape his course. The other method is merely to give him the general direction by a compass he carries. The compass always shows one immutable direction, and therefore shows him every deviation he makes from the right line.

The first method of moral guidance is to give definite external rules. Certain actions are defined, and man is told that he should, or should not, perform them.

"Observe the Sabbath," "Be circumcised," "Do not steal," "Do not drink intoxicants," "Do not take life," "Give tithes to the poor," "Wash and pray five times a day," "Be baptized," "Take communion," etc. Such are the injunctions of external religious teachings, Brahmanist, Buddhist, Mohammedan, or Jewish, and of the Church teaching, miscalled—Christian.

The other method is that of pointing out to man a perfection he cannot attain, but which he is conscious of striving toward. An ideal is pointed out, by referring to which man can always recognize the degree of his own deviation from the right course.

Love thy God with all thy heart, and with all thy soul, and with all thy mind, and thy neighbor as thyself! Be ye perfect as your Father in heaven is perfect! Such is Christ's teaching.

The proof of obedience to the external religious teachings lies in the concurrence of our actions with their injunctions. And such concurrence is possible.

The proof of obedience to Christ's teaching lies in a consciousness of our falling short of ideal perfection. The degree of advance is not seen, but the divergence from perfection is seen.

A man professing an external law is a man standing in the light of a lamp fixed to a post. He stands in the light and sees clearly, but has nowhere to advance to. A man following Christ's teaching is like a man carrying a lantern before him at the end of a pole. The light is ever before him, and ever impels him to follow it, by continually lighting up fresh ground and attracting him onward.

The Pharisee[4] thanks God that he has done his whole duty. The rich young man has also done all from his youth upward, and does not understand what he yet lacks. Nor can they think otherwise. There is nothing before them toward which they might press on. Tithes are paid; Sabbaths observed; parents honored; adultery, theft, murder, avoided. What more? For the follower of Christ's teaching, the attainment of each step toward perfection evokes the need of reaching a still higher step, whence another, higher yet, is revealed, and so on without end. The follower of Christ's law is always in the position of the publican.[5] He is always conscious of his imperfections, not looking back at the road he has already traveled, but always seeing before him the road he has still to go,—over which he has not yet journeyed.

Therein Christ's teaching differs from all other religious teachings. It is not that the demands are different, but the manner of guiding people is different.

Christ did not legislate. He never established any institutions, and never instituted marriage. But men, accustomed to external teachings, and not understanding the nature of Christ's teaching, wished to feel themselves justified, as the Pharisee felt himself justified. And, in contradiction to the whole spirit of Christ's teaching, they concocted, out of its letter, an external code of rules called Church Doctrine, and supplanted Christ's true teaching of the ideal by this doctrine.

In relation to all the occurrences of life, the Church doctrine (calling itself Christian) supplied, instead of Christ's ideal teaching, definitions and rules contrary to the spirit of that teaching. This has been done with reference to government, law, the army, the Church, Church services, and it has been done in regard to marriage. Although Christ not only never instituted marriage, but, if we must seek for external regulations, rather repudiated it ("leave thy wife and follow me"[6]), the Church doctrine (professing to be Christian) has established marriage as a Christian institution. That is to say, it has defined certain external conditions under which sexual love is said to be quite innocent and right for a Christian.

But as in Christ's teaching there is no basis for the institution of marriage, it has resulted that people in our world have left one bank but have not reached the other. That is to say, they do not really believe in the Church definition of marriage, for they feel that such an institution has no basis in Christian teaching; but yet they do not discern Christ's ideal of complete chastity which the Church teaching hides, and they are thus left without guidance in sexual matters. And this explains the seemingly strange fact that among Jews, Mohammedans, Lamaists,[7] and others, following religious teachings of a far lower grade than the Christian, but having exact external definitions of marriage, the family basis and conjugal fidelity is far more firmly established than in so-called Christian society.

Those people have a definite system of concubinage and polygamy and polyandry confined within certain limits. Among us complete dissoluteness exists: concubinage, polygamy, and polyandry confined by no limits and screened under the forms of monogamy.

Merely because the clergy, for money, perform a certain ceremony (called the marriage service) over some of those who come together, it is naïvely, or hypocritically, supposed that we are a monogamous people.

Christian marriage never existed or could exist, any more than Christian worship,[8] or Christian teachers and fathers of the Church, or Christian property, or Christian armies, or law courts, or governments. And this was understood by Christians of the first centuries.

The Christian's ideal is love to God and to his neighbor. It is renunciation of self for the service of God and man. But carnal love, marriage, is a serving of self, and is, therefore, at least a hindrance to the service of God and man, and consequently, from the Christian point of view, it is a fall, a sin.

Getting married cannot conduce to the service of God and man, even if the object of the marriage be the continuation of the human race. It is much simpler for people, instead of getting married to produce future children, to save and support those millions of children who are perishing around us for want of food for body and soul. A Christian could only get married without consciousness of a fall into sin, if he knew that all existing children were already provided for.

It is possible to reject Christ's teaching, that teaching which impregnates our whole life, and on which all our morality is based, but if we accept it, it is impossible not to recognize that it points to the ideal of complete chastity.

In the Gospels it is said plainly, and so that it cannot be explained away: first, that a husband should not divorce his wife in order to take another,[9] but should live with her to whom he has united himself. Secondly, that it is sinful for any one (consequently for a married as well as for an unmarried man) to look on a woman as an object of pleasure.[10] And thirdly, that it is better for the unmarried not to marry at all, *i.e.,* to be perfectly chaste.[11]

To very many people these thoughts will seem strange and even contradictory. And they are indeed contradictory, though not among themselves. The contradiction is to the whole tenor of our lives, and involuntarily a doubt arises: which is right? these thoughts, or the lives of millions of people including my own? This feeling I myself experienced intensely, when I was arriving at the convictions I am now expressing. I never expected that the trend of my thoughts would lead me to such a result as they actually brought me to. I was frightened at my own conclusions, and wished not to believe them, but there was no way to avoid them. And, however these conclusions may contradict the whole tenor of our lives, however much they contradict what I formerly thought and even expressed, I had to accept them.

"But all these are general considerations which may be correct, but which refer to Christ's teachings, and are binding only on those who profess that teaching. But life is life, and it will not do merely to indicate Christ's unattainable ideal ahead of us, and to leave men with nothing but that ideal, and with no definite guidance on a question so burning, so general, and which causes such tremendous misfortunes.

"A young and passionate man will be, at first, attracted by the ideal, but will fail to hold to it and will stumble. And not knowing, and not professing any rules, he will fall into utter depravity."

Thus do people generally argue.

"Christ's ideal is unattainable, and therefore cannot serve to guide us in life; one may talk of it, dream of it, but it is inapplicable to life, and so we must abandon it. What we require is not an ideal, but a precept. A guidance which should correspond to our strength, and suit the average moral strength of our society; an honest Church marriage; or even a marriage not quite honest, in which one of the partners (as the men in our society) may have had intercourse with other partners; or, say, civil marriage; or even (continuing along the same road) a Japanese marriage for a term,—and why not go on till we reach the brothel?"

It is maintained to be preferable to street vice. And this is just the difficulty. Once allow yourself to lower the ideal to suit man's weakness, and there is no finding any limit at which to stop.

But the fact is that such reasoning is false from the very start. It is not true that the ideal of infinite perfection cannot be a guide in life; and that it is necessary, either to throw it up, saying that it is useless to me as I cannot reach it, or else to tone it down to a level that suits my weakness.

Such reasoning is as if a mariner were to say to himself: "Because I cannot keep to the line indicated by my compass, I will cease to look at it and will throw it overboard" (*i.e.,* will reject the ideal), or else, "I will fasten the needle of the compass in the position which corresponds to the direction in which I am at present sailing" (*i.e.,* will lower the ideal to suit my weakness).

The ideal of perfection given by Christ is not a fantasy, or an object for rhetorical sermons; but it is the most essential guide to moral life any man can have. It is like the compass, which is the most necessary and accessible instrument for the guidance of mariners. Only the former must be trusted as implicitly as the latter.

In whatever position a man may be, Christ's teaching of the ideal is always sufficient to furnish him with the surest guidance as to what he should—and should not—do. But he must trust that teaching completely, and that teaching alone, ceasing to follow any other, just as the steersman must trust to the compass and desist from watching what is on either hand, and from guiding himself by such observations.

To guide oneself by Christ's teachings, or by the compass, one must know how to make use of them. To this end it is above all necessary to be conscious of one's position. We must not be afraid to define precisely how far we have deviated from the line of perfection. There is no position in which man can say that he has reached it, and has nothing more to strive toward.

Such is the case concerning man's efforts to reach the Christian ideal in general, and the same is true about chastity in particular. If we imagine to ourselves people in the most diverse positions, with reference to the sex-question, from innocent childhood to marriage of an incontinent character, Christ's teaching, and the ideal he has shown us, will always, at each step between the two, supply clear and definite guidance as to what should, or should not, be done.

What should a pure lad or girl do? Keep themselves pure and free from temptation in order to devote their full powers to the service of God and man, strive after complete chastity in thought and wish.

"What should a youth, or girl, do who has fallen into temptation and is engrossed by vague desire, or by love of some one, and who has thus lost some part of their capacity to serve God and man?"

Exactly the same. Not yield to sin (knowing that yielding will not free them from temptation, but will only increase it); and strive ever toward more and more of chastity, in order to be able more completely to serve God and man.

"What are those to do who have failed in the struggle and have fallen?"

Consider their fall not as a legitimate pleasure (as it is now regarded when justified by a marriage ceremony), nor as a casual pleasure which may be repeated with others, nor as a misfortune, when the fall has occurred with an inferior and without a ceremony; but consider the first fall as the only one, as an entry into actual and indissoluble marriage.

This entry into marriage, by the consequent birth of children, restricts those who are thus united to a new and more limited form of service to God and man. Before marriage they were free to serve God and man directly and in most varied ways. Marriage narrows their scope of action, and demands from them the rearing and educating of offspring, who may serve God and man in the future.

"What should a man and woman do who are married, and who, in accordance with that position, are performing this limited service of God and man, by rearing and educating children?"

Again the same thing. Together strive to be free from temptation. Try to cleanse themselves from the sin of their mutual relation, which hinders general and individual service of God and man; and seek to replace sexual love by the pure relationship of brother and sister.

And so it is not true that we cannot be guided by Christ's ideal, because of its being too lofty, complete, and unattainable.

If we cannot make use of it, this is only because we lie to ourselves and deceive ourselves. For if we say that we must have some rule more practicable than Christ's ideal, or else not reaching Christ's ideal, we shall become vicious,—we do not really say that Christ's ideal is too high for us, but merely that we do not believe in it, and do not want to define our actions by it. To say that when once we have fallen, we shall have begun a loose life, is merely to state that we have decided beforehand that to fall with one who is a social inferior is not a sin, but only an amusement, a distraction, which need not be remedied by the permanent union of marriage. Whereas, if we understood that such a fall is indeed a sin, which must and can be redeemed only by indissoluble marriage, and by all the activity resulting from the birth of children in marriage, then the fall would certainly not be the cause of our plunging into vice.

To act otherwise would be as if a husbandman learning to sow were to abandon a field he had sown badly, and go on sowing a second and a third field, and were to take into account only the one field which succeeded. Evidently such a man would waste much land and seed, and would not learn to sow properly.

Keep but in view the ideal of chastity, and consider every fall (no matter whose or with whom) as the one, immutable lifelong marriage, and it will be clear that the guidance given by Christ is not only sufficient, but is the only guidance possible.

It is said, "Man is weak, and more should not be demanded of him than he can accomplish." But this is like saying, "My hand is weak, I cannot draw the straight line I wish to, therefore, to make it easier, I will take a crooked or broken line as my model." Really, the weaker my hand, the more am I in need of a perfect model.

It is impossible, having heard Christ's ideal teaching, to act as if we knew it not, and to replace it by external ordinances. Christ's ideal teaching is before humanity now just because it is suitable for our guidance in man's present stage of development. Humanity has outgrown the period of external religious ordinances—they are no longer believed in.

The Christian teaching of the ideal is the only one that can guide humanity. We neither can nor may replace Christ's ideal by external rules; but we must firmly keep this ideal before us in all its purity, and above all, we must trust it.

While the mariner sailed near the shore it was possible to say to him, "Keep to that cliff, cape, or tower." But a time comes when the ship is far from shore, and it should and can be guided only by the unattainable star and the compass indicating a direction.

And both are given us.

NOTES

THE KREUTZER SONATA

1. *Under his overcoat . . . were visible a sleeveless kaftan:* a mistake in the translation, perhaps, since a kaftan (both in Persia and in Russia) is worn on the outside. The word in Russian is поддёвка (*podyovka*), a waistcoat (worn beneath an overcoat, usually sleeveless). Moreover, "kaftan" tends to orientalize the story.

2. Domostroy: very well known sixteenth-century corpus of advice on household management and mores compiled by the monk Sylvester. It held great sway over traditional Russian culture at least until Peter the Great's reforms of the early eighteenth century.

3. *marshal of the nobility:* an elected position created by Catherine the Great's Charter of the Nobility (1785). It provided the gentry a very circumscribed form of representational government when dealing with the czar on issues pertaining to the management of districts and provinces, chiefly property rights for the gentry.

4. *Rigolboche:* pseudonym for Amélie Marguerite Badel, a notorious French danseuse to whom the cancan, an informal dance based on the quadrille, is attributed. Her nickname is derived from the French word *rigolo*, "funny," "silly."

5. *I showed her my diary:* a mistake Tolstoy himself made in 1862 when he showed his eighteen-year-old fiancée, Sofya Andreyevna Bers, his diaries, which likewise detailed his premarital dalliances.

6. *the Schopenhauers and Hartmanns, and the Buddhists:* Arthur Schopenhauer (1788–1860), German philosopher whose book *The World as Will and Idea* promoted the idea that abnegation of the will to live was the highest moral aim of man. Eduard von Hartmann (1842–1906) continued Schopenhauer's philosophical pessimism and likewise championed the idea of human will as the ultimate source of unhappiness and discord in the

world. The Buddhists believe that the highest bliss, Nirvana, is coincident with the negation of the self.

7. *Charcot:* Jean-Martin Charcot (1825–93), French physician, teacher, and one of the founders of modern neurology. His neurological clinic in the Salpêtrière hospital, in Paris, was internationally famous during the second half of the nineteenth century.

8. *Phrynes:* Phryne, a famous courtesan of fourth-century Greece.

9. *Truba and Grachevka:* streets in Moscow infamous for the prostitutes who openly plied their trade.

10. *Uriah's wife:* Bathsheba, who was seduced by King David while married to Uriah the Hittite. David had Uriah killed and then married Bathsheba.

11. *They played Beethoven's* Kreutzer Sonata: also known as Beethoven's Violin Sonata in A Major, it was completed and premiered in 1803.

12. "Yes, good-bye . . . forgive me": "Forgive me" and "farewell" are related words in Russian. Pozdnyshev says *prostite,* which primarily means "forgive," but it was also an archaistic way (in late-nineteenth-century Russian) to say "farewell." Compare Pozdnyshev's last words to those of Ivan Ilyich in *The Death of Ivan Ilyich* or to the words of the injured soldier at the end of Tolstoy's story "Sevastopol in December."

SEQUEL TO THE KREUTZER SONATA

Biblical citations from New American Standard Bible.

1. Sequel to The Kreutzer Sonata: an intentional mistranslation by Thomas Crowell. The correct translation for the piece is "An Afterword to *The Kreutzer Sonata.*"

2. *spears into pruning-hooks:* "And they will hammer their swords into plowshares and their spears into pruning hooks" (Isa. 2:4).

3. *lions shall lie down with the lambs:* Tolstoy gets his animals mixed up, since Isaiah prophesies a day when "the wolf will dwell with the lamb and the leopard will lie down with the young goat and the calf and the young lion and the fatling together" (Isa. 11:6).

4. *Pharisee:* member of an ancient Jewish sect that strictly observed the traditional and written law.

5. *in the position of the publican:* Matt. 18:17 instructs the reader to treat the incorrigibly sinful the same way one would treat "a pagan or a tax collector." A publican thus came to mean someone cut off from the Church.

6. *"leave thy wife and follow me":* presumably a reference to a variant redaction that adds "wife" to the list in Matt. 19:29: "And everyone who has left houses or brothers or sisters or father or mother or children or fields for my sake will receive a hundred times as much and will inherit eternal life."

7. *Lamaist:* a Tibetan Buddhist who acknowledges the Dalai Lama as an incarnated deity.

8. *any more than Christian worship:* a reference to several passages in the Gospels that seem to contraindicate organized worship for Christians, most notably: "When you pray, you are not to be like the hypocrites; for they love to stand and pray in the synagogues and on the street corners so that they may be seen by men. Truly I say to you, they have their reward in full. But you, when you pray, go into your inner room, close your door and pray to your Father who is in secret, and your Father who sees what is done in secret will reward you" (Matt. 6:5–6).

9. *that a husband should not divorce . . . to take another:* "It was said, 'whoever sends his wife away, let him give her a certificate of divorce'; but I say to you that everyone who divorces his wife, except for the reason of unchastity, makes her commit adultery; and whoever marries a divorced woman commits adultery" (Matt. 5:31–32).

10. *it is sinful . . . object of pleasure:* "You have heard that it was said, 'You shall not commit adultery'; but I say to you that everyone who looks at a woman with lust for her has already committed adultery with her in his heart" (Matt. 5:27–28).

11. *to be perfectly chaste:* "The disciples said to Him, 'If the relationship of the man with his wife is like this, it is better not to marry.' But He said to them, 'Not all men can accept this statement, but only those to whom it has been given. For there are eunuchs who were born that way from their mother's womb; and there are eunuchs who were made eunuchs by men; and there are also eunuchs who made themselves eunuchs for the sake of the kingdom of heaven. He who is able to accept this, let him accept it" (Matt. 19:10–12).

READING GROUP GUIDE

1. The publication of *The Kreutzer Sonata* was a significant intellectual event around the world. Its publication, at the beginning of the 1890s, set off an explosive debate in Europe, America, and Asia on matters that were then called the "sexual question" and the "woman problem." Its provocative rejoinders to these debates stirred widespread condemnation from all sides, as well as fervent admiration. Moreover, almost everywhere (including the United States), *The Kreutzer Sonata* was censored or forbidden as "indecent literature." Put yourself into the shoes of the average reader in the 1890s. What do you think people found offensive or indecent about Pozdnyshev's views? How has the time between the novella's initial publication and the time that you are reading it changed the ways in which readers react to the ideas? Which of Pozdnyshev's views on women's rights, sex, marriage, and love are still relevant? Which are irrelevant?

2. It has often been noted that Tolstoy, like many other nineteenth-century novelists, constantly returned to the problem of free will in his works. That is to say that Tolstoy examined and illustrated the context and process of ethical decision making, asking to what extent circumstances influence our choices, and to what ex-

tent our actions are unconstrained by circumstances. *The Kreutzer Sonata* deals with this question of free will in Pozdnyshev's explanation to the curious narrator as to why he murdered his own wife. To what extent does Pozdnyshev take responsibility for the murder? Who else shares guilt? How convincing is Pozdnyshev's explanation for how and why the murder happened?

3. The novella's first epigraph is Christ's injunction against looking lustfully, from the Sermon on the Mount: "But I say unto you, That whosoever looketh on a woman to lust after her hath committed adultery with her already in his heart" (Matt. 5:28). Why would Tolstoy choose, as an epigraph to a novel entitled after a work of music, a biblical verse that deals directly with the act of looking? In what ways does the novella reflect the concerns of the epigraph?

4. In *The Kreutzer Sonata* and other works by Tolstoy, especially those he wrote after his religious conversion in the 1870s, one frequently finds statements that have been described as "flagrantly misogynistic." However, at the time of its publication, *The Kreutzer Sonata* was viewed by many supporters of the women's rights movement as supporting their cause, especially the remarks Pozdnyshev makes about child care, pregnancy, and sexual inequality. Moreover, later critics have noted that Pozdnyshev's views have much in common with feminist critiques from the 1960s and 1970s. For example, Pozdnyshev remarks, "Well, and now they emancipate woman, they give her all the same rights as man, but they still regard her as an instrument of enjoyment, so they educated her, both in childhood and later by public opinion, with this end in view. But she remains the same depraved slave as ever before. . . ." Discuss Tolstoy's (or, perhaps more correctly, Pozdnyshev's) views in the context of your own experience and knowledge of feminism and women's rights movements. Is Tolstoy a misogynist? A champion of women's rights? A radical or a conservative? What solutions does Tolstoy offer to the "woman problem"?

5. *The Kreutzer Sonata* has often been criticized and dismissed for being "utopian," as advocating impossibly ideal social and politi-

cal schemes. What examples of utopianism can you find in the text?

6. In the *Sequel to The Kreutzer Sonata,* Tolstoy repeatedly makes reference to verses from the Gospels as evidence supporting his views. He claims to offer a more accurate interpretation of the intent of the New Testament and Jesus' teachings than is offered by "official" Christianity. He argues, for instance, that the teachings of the Gospels forbid marriage, church services, priests, property, taxes, armies, courts, and government. Read the full text of the verses he cites (given in the endnotes to this edition, though you might also read other translations and redactions). How fair and accurate are Tolstoy's conclusions? How does Tolstoy reconcile traditional Christian practice and interpretation with the literal text of the Bible?

A Note on the Type

The principal text of this Modern Library edition
was set in a digitized version of Janson, a typeface that
dates from about 1690 and was cut by Nicholas Kis,
a Hungarian working in Amsterdam. The original matrices have
survived and are held by the Stempel foundry in Germany.
Hermann Zapf redesigned some of the weights and sizes for
Stempel, basing his revisions on the original design.